Inklings Book 2019

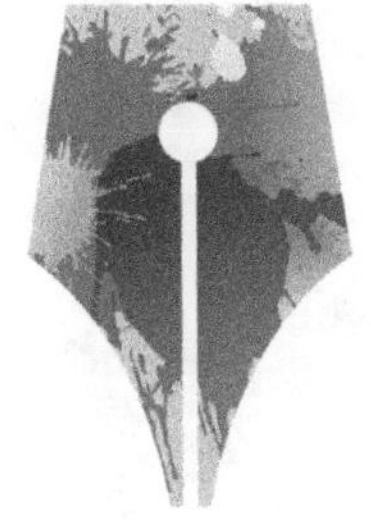

The following young authors contributed their short stories and poems to this anthology.

Maryam Ali	Kaia Lucas	Julie Shi
Vedant Balan	Ching Yi Mak	Caroline Strickland
Simon Chien	Chris L. Matthews, II	Esabella Uche
Maizie Ferguson	Austin Moon	Natalie Wong
Inés Garcia	Sanjay Ravishankar	Melody Xu
Maia Goel	Claire Reiger	Caitlyn Zhu
	Carolina Ruiz	Liana Zhu

Thank you to the following mentors for contributing editorial guidance and letters.

Davorah Berman	Ailynn Knox-Collins	Megan White
Bronté Bettencourt	Tasslyn Magnusson	Kristi Wright
Philomena Block	Jena McNealy	
Malar Ganapathiappan	Kalena Miller	
Julia Hettiger	Melody Reed	
Ellen Kazimer	Beth Spencewood	

Cover illustration by Polly Alice McCann (www.pollymadison.com)
Copyedited by Tasslyn Magnusson
Edited by Naomi Kinsman

Printed in the USA
First Printing: August 2019
ISBN: 978-0-9981849-6-8

Contents

Thank you to our Collaborating Artists!

John David Anderson

Kerry Aradhya

Kati Bartkowski

Rebecca Behrens

Ashley Herring Blake

Joanna Ho Bradshaw

David Butler

Kheryn Callender

Ernesto Cisneros

Kim Culbertson

Jill Davis

Mandy Davis

Sharon M. Draper

Lisa Greenwald

Marilyn Hilton

Ann Jacobus

Heidi Lang

Beth McMullen

Patricia Newman

Daria Peoples-Riley

Mitali Perkins

Shannon Price

Helen Pyne

Raina Telgemeier

Elizabeth Verdick

Ashley Walker

Pam Watts

Kristi Wright

Anne Young

Foreword

We can't wait to share this literary feast with you, our eleventh annual *Inklings Book*! Since 2008, Society of Young Inklings has hosted the Inklings Book Contest annually, a free opportunity for youth writers to work with author-mentors to polish their stories and poems.

Our focus in this book—in fact, our focus in the entire Inklings Book Contest—is revision. Lots of authors, no matter their age, find revision challenging. Some even wonder: *Is revision necessary?* Why revise, if your work is already strong enough to win a contest? At SYI, our author-mentors have experienced for themselves that the question, "How might I make my writing stronger?" always yields interesting results. Instead of looking for mistakes, we're looking for opportunities. In the interviews to come, you'll hear from the youth published in this book about their discoveries as they looked at revision through the lens of "What's possible?"

Readers beware! You may just find yourself wanting to take on a revision of your own as you dig into this book. If so, check out the "Dear Reader" letters from each author-mentor, explaining the revision strategy chosen for their mentees. Whether you're an educator, a young writer, or an author yourself, we hope you'll find inspiration in these letters—and in the insightful, imaginative work that follows them.

The twenty stories and poems in this anthology were dreamed into being by writers in grades three through nine, and feature treasure seekers, a magic-snatching villain, beloved pets, Greek gods, and above all, encouragement to youth writers everywhere to tap into their powerful voices and share them with the world.

If you're interested in becoming an Inkling yourself, or one of our Collaborating Artists, you can sign up for a free Society of Young Inklings membership at *www.younginklings.org*. While you're there, feel free to browse our mentorship opportunities, online courses, writing prompts, author interviews, and other offerings. We appreciate you being part of our community!

Intriguing Beginnings

Jena McNealy worked with Esabella Uche on creating an intriguing beginning to draw the reader into Esabella's story, *Miraculous*.

Dear Reader,

When I read Esabella's story *Miraculous*, I was intrigued. Esabella's descriptive details made me feel like I was right there in the story with the main character. But the story was very long. The beginning didn't hook me in as much as the middle and end. We decided to focus on creating an intriguing beginning as we revised.

Esabella had an open mind when it came to revising. She was able to condense her story drastically by removing scenes that weren't important to the main story line. Her new beginning hooks you right into the story.

When revising a story for length, look at the story as a whole and work on focusing your reader's attention where you want it. Are there any scenes that can be shortened or removed?

Try giving each of your scenes a fitting title. Then, write each scene title on a separate index card. Lay out your cards as a storyboard. Once you can see your scenes more clearly, you can figure out what's most important to the story and what isn't so important. That way, you can choose where to focus your reader's attention and where you want to move the reader quickly forward to the next important detail or scene. Also, if a scene isn't important to the main problem of the story, you may even be able to take it out completely.

You may find it difficult to figure out where scenes start and end. If this happens for you, imagine your story as a play. Where would the lights come up to start a scene? Where might they black out? You'll find scene breaks often happen when characters move from one setting to another. If you have long passages that list things happening, but which aren't truly scenes, try turning what's most important in the list into a scene. Expanding summary into a scene or two is another way to make a story stronger.

Enjoy the story!

Jena McNealy

Jena McNealy has always had a passion for education. She enjoys writing children's books and teaching preschool. Jena believes that all young learners deserve the opportunity to explore their creative potential. Jena holds a B.A in Creative Arts and a minor in Education from San Jose State University. In her spare time, Jena enjoys traveling and cooking.

Esabella Uche

Esabella says: "I'm eight years old and in the third grade. My favorite colors are white and black. My favorite food is sushi. I have two unique talents. I can throw my feet all the way above my head and I can make my tongue look like a four-leaf clover. I like to read fantasy and adventure stories. I like to write whatever comes to my mind."

Jena McNealy: When did you start writing?
Esabella Uche: I started writing when I was in first grade. My stories weren't very good, but I keep improving each year.

Q: How did you get the idea for *Miraculous*?
A: It was a school assignment. We received three random words and had to create a sentence with the words. My words were red, coffee, and Africa. After writing the sentence, I started writing the story.

Q: Where do you like to write?
A: I don't really care where I write as long as it's quiet. When it's quiet, I can think of more ideas.

Q: What advice do you have for other Young Inklings who don't like revision very much?
A: If you don't like revising, try just a looking at a little part of the story. Revising is important if you want your readers to read a good story. So my advice is to start small.

Miraculous

by

Esabella Uche

CHAPTER ONE

"Ring, ring," sounded the bell.

Chidima jumped off her bike as fast as she could. She didn't want to be late for school. Quickly, she locked her bike to the bike rack and ran up the school steps. Around her kids were talking excitedly. She pushed through the crowd until she found her locker. She was just about to open it when she heard a familiar voice.

"Hi Chidima," said Jessie.

"Hey Jessie, late too?" said Chidima.

"Me? Never!" she said with a little laugh.

Once they got to the library they started to walk down the aisles of books.

"So, which book are you gonna get?" Chidima asked as they stopped every now and then to look at some of the entertaining covers on display.

"Well, the teacher did say we have an informational report we

have to do. We should try to look for some informational books," said Jessie.

Good idea, Chidima thought. *What do I want to write a report about anyway? Cats? Dogs? How about Nigeria? I've always wanted to go visit and maybe doing a report about it will help me learn more.*

Chidima went to the aisle where she had seen books on different countries. She ran her finger over the spines until finally she found one.

This looks pretty good, she thought.

The book had just been published and it had a cool font on the cover. Just as she was waiting and thinking about where Jessie was, her friend came over with her own book in hand.

"So, which book did you get, Chidima?" asked Jessie.

"I got a book on…" Chidima hid the book behind her back.

She was a little embarrassed about her book selection. She didn't want to broadcast it for her classmates around her to hear.

"I got a book about Nigeria," Chidima said shyly. "I'm going to include some of the newest facts in my report so it's not boorrrinng," said Chidima with an exaggerated eye roll.

"Nice," said Jessie.

"How about you Jess, what you get?" Chidima inquired.

"I got a book on technology and gadgets. It's about how all of these cool gadgets are made," Jessie declared.

"Wow! I wish I understood all that stuff. Maybe you could teach me some time," said Chidima.

Jess just smiled and they both took their place in line. Chidima took a glimpse out of the window. She saw what looked like grey, heavy, rain clouds.

Oh no, she thought.

She hadn't checked the weather report before she left home and she was going to get stuck without an umbrella. Chidima dreaded the thought of riding her bike home from school in the wet rain but there was no other way around it.

CHAPTER TWO

Once home Chidima leaned against the front door and let out a huge sigh of relief. She was drenched from head to toe. As she began to walk to her room, out ran her little sister, Joy.

"Chidima! You're wet everywhere. Why'd that happen to you?" Joy asked excitedly.

"I forgot my raincoat and umbrella," Chidima admitted, embarrassed. "Did you have a fun day today, Joy?" Chidima asked, trying to change the subject quickly.

"Yup! I got a new coloring book and crayons," Joy said as if it was the best thing in the world. "Wanna see?"

"Maybe later, okay? I gotta get out of these clothes!" Chidima exclaimed. Joy took one more perplexed look at Chidima and then ran off to the living room.

Once Chidima got out of the shower, she grabbed her backpack and took out her notes from school that day. She took out her book on Nigeria and started to read. She learned that some of the richest people in Africa live in Nigeria. She also learned that some people lived in poverty. There were many children who suffered and didn't get proper food. There were also problems in Nigeria related to children not being able to use their degrees once they graduated.

Apparently, there was a lot of corruption the book said. Many as half the people lived below the poverty line. The thought made Chidima shudder. She wasn't rich by any means here in America but at least she and her family got by.

Chidima started to think maybe visiting Nigeria wasn't all it was cracked up to be. Her dad said they had family over there and she always wanted to visit but after reading about the country she didn't want to go so much anymore.

In the midst of her thoughts, a huge lightning bolt ripped through the sky. Chidima was startled for a moment. She tried to keep reading but it was difficult to concentrate with the lightning continuing to flash. Chidima decided it was too dangerous to sit by the window and closed her book. She went to the other side of the room to take a break, flopping down on her bed with a sense of relief. Chidima thought about what kind of personality the rain would have if it could speak. On one hand, she thought it was playful, but then on the other hand maybe it was angry.

She thought about how she was going to sleep amidst the thunderstorm. It was pretty scary and she was starting to feel a little afraid. There were little lightning bolts and then every few seconds there was a really loud one. The storm went on and on like this for about 30 minutes and then finally ... it stopped. Chidima waited for a few minutes before she went to look out the window. She peered through the side of the shade, too afraid to look straight out of the window. There was a calm peace that radiated from the rain. A light drizzle was still falling but it made her feel peaceful more than anything else. Feeling comforted, she climbed in her bed and drifted quickly off to sleep.

CHAPTER THREE

"Wake up Chidima! Wake up. Dad says he has important news for us," Joy said excitedly.

Chidima pulled the covers down slowly so she could see Joy's face. One look at Joy's face told her she was serious, so Chidima tossed her blanket aside and put her house slippers on. She walked to the kitchen with Joy by her side.

"I understand. Certainly. Okay, see you soon," she heard her mother say as she hung up the phone.

"What's wrong?" Chidima asked.

"Bad news Chidima," her mother said. "You know your grandmother from your Dad's side? Well, she has come down with a life-threatening illness. She is not expected to make it past the month. Your dad wants to fly us to Nigeria so we can see her one final time," her mother said.

"Wow, I'm so sorry," Chidima said.

I never even met my grandmother before, she thought.

"Well, we are leaving tonight. So, you need to pack your bags and bring enough for one week." Her mom motioned to the calendar for extra emphasis. "Don't worry about school. I called them already and you will be fine," her mom added.

"Okay, mom," Chidima said.

Chidima walked to her room with a feeling of excitement and anxiety at the same time. She had always wanted to visit Nigeria but she remembered what she read last night in her library book. She was afraid even though they had family there. Chidima pushed those thoughts aside and started packing her bags.

CHAPTER FOUR

"We are now approaching Lagos. Please be mindful of your overhead baggage as you exit the plane!"

Chidima couldn't believe she was finally here…in Africa. It was her first time out of United States. The plane flight had taken a long eighteen hours. Chidima, Joy, her mom, and dad exited the plane and walked into the terminal of Murtala Muhammed airport. Chidima was surprised to see most of the faces of the people were black. That was something she didn't see regularly back in her hometown. In a sense, it was comforting. She liked how the people seemed so cheery and helpful.

Her dad found a taxi cab and they all piled into car. Chidima got into the back seat of the taxi and looked at the view as they drove along. Apparently, they were driving down the main road and it was busy and bustling. There was an open-air market with fruit and vegetable sellers, others were fixing watches or selling cell phones. It looked like things had been this way for a long time and the market had a certain flow to it as if everyone knew what to do. Chidima kept thinking maybe she could ask her mom to take her shopping there soon.

After ten minutes of driving in the taxi, the car pulled up a long, narrow dirt road. There were very scanty houses that looked very old and as if they were about to fall apart any minute. Her dad paid the taxi driver with foreign looking money again and waved goodbye as he went back down the road.

"I didn't realize our family here in Nigeria was so poor," Chidima said.

"Unfortunately, it's true Chidima," her dad said. "Some families are wealthy and live on the mainland, but most wealthy people in Nigeria tend to live on islands. There is a lot of criminal activity where your grandmother lives during the evening so it's best you stay indoors until we leave to go back home. Don't worry, your grandmother has a small back yard for you and your sister to play in."

"Okay, Dad," Chidima said in a rather sullen tone.

She was hoping to get out and experience more of Nigeria but it was starting to look like she might get stuck in the house all day. As they neared her grandmother's house, right next door she saw a group of young children playing tag with each other. Their clothes were ragged and a little dirty, but despite that they looked like they didn't know and were having a great time with each other. She envied them a little for a moment.

On the other side of the dirt road was a man who looked quite poor. He was sitting down with his bike and was writing in a note pad. He looked happy and content. As Chidima looked around she focused in on her grandmother's house. It was made of steel and had a silvery surface. It looked poor and Chidima let out a disappointed grimace when she saw it. Her dad knocked on the door and a young-looking woman opened it.

"Oh my! she exclaimed. "You're here already! I haven't seen you for ages. How are you, brother?"

Her dad, a little tired from the long trip, said, "Under the circumstances, doing well. Please, meet my family. This is my wife and two daughters, Joy and Chidima."

"Hello, so nice to meet you. I am sorry if my English is not the best. Please come in and sit. Would you like a drink?"

"Yes," Chidima said.

Her dad's sister went to the kitchen to fix drinks for everyone. When she returned, she handed her dad a drink first, then her mom, and finally Chidima and Joy in that order.

"Chidima, this drink is called Zobo. It comes from a plant. It is a popular drink here in Nigeria. It tastes a little like juice and tea mixed together."

"Thank you," Chidima said.

She tasted the drink and it was pretty good. It didn't taste like anything she'd had before.

"Where's Mother?" her dad asked.

"Follow me. She is in the other room." The family followed her to the back room.

Chidima's grandmother was in bed in her nightgown with her head propped up with pillows. She looked comfortable but also quite pale.

"Mother, hello. How are you doing?"

Chidima's grandmother opened her eyes a little and looked. She squinted and then began to smile,

"Not too good, not too good," she said shaking her head sadly. "I can barely get out of bed these days."

Chidima was surprised that she spoke English. It was English with an accent, but still understandable.

Her grandmother looked at the family and a warm expression went over her face. "Is this your family?"

"Yes, this is my wife and these are my two daughters, Joy and Chidima."

"Hi, little one. Can you give me some sugar?" her grandmother asked.

"What sugar?" Joy said.

"That's how they say it in America, no? It's a hug and kiss," she explained.

"Okay," Joy walked over and gave her grandma a big hug and kiss.

"Thank you so much. That was the best hug ever," her grandmother said, her face softening.

"Chidima, is that you?"

"Yes, Grandma. It's me, Chidima."

"Yes, that's a lovely name," her grandmother said. "Do you know that Chi means God in Nigeria? I believe your name means… She paused for a second…*God is good.*"

"Wow, I didn't know. I never really thought about it," said Chidima.

"Your aunt here, her name is Chinasa and that means *God answers.* You also have a cousin here in Nigeria and her name is Chinyere that means *God gives.* Your name is unique and beautiful Chidima. Don't ever be ashamed of it."

"Okay, Grandma. I won't." Chidima said.

"Mom, do you need some rest?" her aunt said.

"Yes, a little. Give me a few hours to rest. I'll call for you if I need you."

Her aunt ushered everyone out of the room and back into the front living room. She led the family down a short hallway and showed Joy and Chidima the room they would be sharing.

"I know it's a little small, but it will have to do," her aunt said.

Chidima walked into a small room with two beds, a dresser,

and a few plants. Some pictures hung on the wall for decoration.

Chidima began to unpack their bags and started to talk to Joy. "Are you excited to be here, Joy?"

"Mmmhmm!" Joy had found a little bouncy ball toy and was busy playing with it.

After unpacking her bags and Joy's, Chidima plopped down on the bed and took out her library book on Nigeria. It was a little funny to Chidima that she was here in Nigeria reading her library book about Nigeria. She thought maybe there would be some adventure during her trip here.

She started to read, and for about an hour it was silent. Then, suddenly, it began to rain again. At first, it was soft and then it rained more heavily. Before you know it, there was thunder and lightning. Chidima could feel the thunder and it was just as frightening as it had been in America. She was scared to get close to the window so she backed away to the corner of the room and kept a safe distance.

She looked over to see what Joy was doing. Her sister was asleep in the bed having worn herself out from playing with the toys that were in the room. Chidima went to the other bed and put her head under the covers. She felt safer and stayed there until some of the thunder had died down.

CHAPTER FIVE

Chidima must have dozed off. When she opened her eyes, she realized it wasn't thundering anymore but raining only slightly. She got the courage to peek outside the window like she would back at home. There in her grandmother's own back yard she saw something that she hadn't seen earlier. Amidst the garden and few toys that had been there before, was a tree. And it was not just any tree. There was something different about it. It almost shimmered despite the fact it was dark as night outside. Chidima rubbed her eyes to see if she was imagining it. She opened her eyes again and yep, there it was. She decided she had to get a better look even though it was dark and cold and just a wee bit scary.

Chidima noticed there was a door leading out to the backyard from her room so she opened it and started to walk outside. She walked up to the tree. It looked like a regular tree except it had strange looking red beans hanging from the branches. Chidima wondered if she should touch them or not. She decided to take a chance and she reached out to touch the beans. They were wet and soft but definitely real. Upon closer inspection, the beans looked like coffee beans– reddish-looking coffee beans. Chidima called to her mom and dad to come see the tree also.

"Dad, Mom, Auntie. Come quick!" she yelled at the top of her lungs.

Her mom, dad and aunt ran out to see what the commotion was about. It was something quite unusual for Chidima to be yelling at the top of her lungs.

"What is it, Chidima?" her mom said first.

"It's a tree with red coffee beans on it. It's incredible!" Chidima exclaimed.

"That wasn't here before," her Aunt said incredulously.

As her dad, mom, and aunt circled the tree and started to touch it, they realized it truly was real but no one had any idea how it had gotten there.

CHAPTER SIX

Her dad took some coffee beans from the tree.

"Let's roast them and see how they taste," he said adventurously.

"Okay," her aunt said.

Chidima followed behind them into the kitchen and sat down at the kitchen table. She was curious how the beans would taste and if they were even edible. Her dad placed the coffee beans inside a filter and grinder machine until the beans were ground to a fine powder. As he poured water in the machine and set the power to on, Chidima kept wondering how exactly might this coffee taste. What if it was poisonous? Or what if it was the best-tasting coffee ever? After about ten minutes, her mom placed little mugs on the table, just for her mom and dad.

"The adults have to taste test it first," she said.

Her mom and aunt poured milk on it and her dad drank it plain. They looked at each other nervously and after a small sip her aunt was the first to talk.

"Chidima, this has got to be the best coffee I ever tasted!"

"What do you think?" she elbowed her dad.

"Wow, this coffee is really good. I've never tasted anything like it!" he said.

"Can I try too, Mom?" Chidima asked.

"All right, come get a cup," her mom said.

Chidima ran up to her mom and tried the coffee herself. Her mom gave her a nice helping of milk and sugar and just as the adults had said, she couldn't believe her taste buds. It was sweet and tasty like a chocolate mocha but also a little spicy and fruity like the Zobo drink she had earlier. After some excitement and lots of talk the family decided to get back to bed and figure out what to do with the tree in the morning.

CHAPTER SEVEN

"Oh, my! Oh my!" Chidima heard her aunt exclaim from the other room.

She found her dad, mom and aunt all in her grandmother's room. She saw her aunt sobbing and shaking her head. Her dad was rubbing her back and giving her a shoulder to cry on.

"It's gonna be okay. Don't worry, that's why I'm here. To help you," her dad told her aunt.

As Chidima entered the room the reality of what was happening started to become more apparent. Her grandmother was…dead. In the night, she had died peacefully in her sleep. She lay there motionless with her eyes closed. Chidima felt sad for her grandmother but at the same time she also was happy for her. She had lived a good life until old age. Her life had been filled with love from her family and friends.

"Chidima, your grandmother is no longer here with us. She has gone to a better place. We are going to call the hospital and see what we should do next."

"Okay, Mom. Do you think it is weird that grandma died the same night we found the miracle coffee tree?" Chidima asked.

Chidima's dad stopped to consider what Chidima said. "Maybe it's a blessing from your grandma. Our ancestors always said

the woman in our family line were wise women, women with power. Maybe it's a gift from her," her dad said thoughtfully.

CHAPTER EIGHT

As the days went by Chidima's family was very busy. Her dad started to make funeral arrangements for her grandmother and her aunt and mom were continuing to make use of the coffee beans. Chidima was ecstatic about the whole situation.

Her aunt had an idea. "Why don't we try to give some to the neighbors? If they like the coffee too, then we can know for sure we haven't gone mad. If they like it maybe then we should take it to the local market."

"Okay," her mom said. "I made some coffee this morning with the beans. Let's take a few cups and start with the neighbors here on this street."

Both her mom and her aunt busied themselves with making a tray of various coffee cups. They both walked out of the house on a mission. Chidima wanted to know what was going to happen so she followed them out of the house.

The first person they saw was the man with the bike who always sat down in the afternoons to write in his notebook. Chidima's aunt approached him first. She told him they wanted to taste test a new kind of coffee and wanted his opinion on how it tasted.

The man was surprised but said "Okay, I'll try it." After a few sips he looked back at Chidima's mom and aunt with a surprised look on his face. "Where did you get this coffee? I've never tasted anything like it before."

Chidima's aunt spoke up first and told him it was a "family

secret." She gave Chidima a wink and then they were off to find a new taste tester. They tried just about every adult who lived down that road. Each and every person loved the coffee. Everyone would marvel at its taste and then ask what the secret was to such a good cup of coffee.

Each time her aunt would say, "It's a family secret." After about an hour of taking it to the local neighbors to try, Chidima's aunt said "I'm starting to think we should take this coffee to the local market," her aunt said.

"The only thing is that we leave back for America in two days. We won't be able to see what happens with the beans here in Nigeria. We also would like to bring some coffee beans home to America. Would that be all right with you?" Chidima's mom asked.

"Of course," said her aunt. "Take as much as you need. I will call you on a weekly basis and let you know how everything is going down here. I have a friend here in Nigeria in the oil business. I may be able to call him and ask him to taste test and get some good business advice from him," she said. With that, they all entered Chidima's grandmother's house excited and exhausted from the day's events.

CHAPTER NINE

Two days later Chidima and her family were already packed and ready to go back home to America. They had already given their respects to their grandmother, picked tons of beans from the tree and were currently back at the airport in Nigeria. As their flight number was called, Chidima's aunt kneeled down to hug Joy and then Chidima.

"Chidima, you discovered this coffee tree. Who knows how it

got here, maybe it was your grandmother or maybe it has something to do with you. Either way, I am grateful. Be careful of the beans. They are special. If you ever want to come visit me in Nigeria, you can come whenever you want," she said, emphasizing the word *whenever.*

"Ok, Auntie." Chidima smiled again.

She was sad to leave Nigeria and the excitement that they had there but she knew it would always be in her heart. She was ready to get back home and see what plans her dad and mom had for the coffee beans there.

CHAPTER TEN

Chidima and her family arrived back home in California on a Friday evening.

"Chidima, I want to take some coffee to the local farmers' market tomorrow. Be ready to come with me early in the morning," her dad said.

"Okay, Dad," Chidima said thoughtfully.

She started to wonder how things would go tomorrow. She took her things out of her suitcase; clothes and a little souvenir for herself…a coffee bean from the mysterious tree back in Nigeria. She placed it on her night stand, turned off the light and slept better than she ever had before.

The next morning Chidima and her dad hopped in the car and drove off. About thirty minutes later, they arrived at the farmers' market. Some sellers were setting up their fruit stands and others were setting up vegetable stands. The smell of fresh baked bread and pie hung in the air. Another seller sold homemade soaps and crystals. Her dad approached one of the sellers.

"Is there a manager on site? Who do I speak to about setting up a stand?"

One of the fruit farmers spoke up. "If you go straight down that way by the waterfall you will see there is an office. The manger is there on the weekend and he can tell you everything you need to know."

"Thank you," said Chidima's dad.

Chidima and her dad walked past the waterfall into the market's managerial office. Her dad opened the door for Chidima, and they walked in.

"Hello, anyone here?" her dad asked.

There was no one at the front counter but as soon as she thought that a man with a crisp white shirt and a wide brimmed hat came forward.

"Can I help you?" he asked politely.

"Yes, we have a new product we would like to sell here at the farmers' market," her dad said.

"All right, what is it?" the man said.

"It's a new and fresh tasting coffee from Africa. We brought a sample here today. Would you like to try some?" her dad said.

The man peered down from his hat and looked at Chidima and her dad over a few times.

"Sure, why not," he said after a moment.

Chidima's dad poured coffee into a mug from the coffee container he brought with them. The coffee poured out with a little steam coming from the container. She could tell it was still fresh and warm. The man took the cup and took a sip, and then another and another. Before Chidima could blink her eyes twice he had drunk the entire mug.

"This has got to be the best tasting coffee I ever had," the man said.

"Really?" Chidima and her dad said at the same time, a little incredulously.

"Definitely. Look, I know you are interested in setting up shop here but this coffee could make tons more money in the supermarket. Have you ever thought about selling it there?" the man said.

"The thought crossed my mind," her dad said. "But I don't know where to start."

"Well, let me help you with that. I have the phone number of a man that owns one of the local supermarkets here. I'll give you his number and tell him I recommended you. Here's my card with my contact information. I'd call today. He should be in the office. In the meantime, would you like to set up shop today at our humble farmers' market? This coffee is so good that just for today I'll let you sell it here free of charge," the man said.

"Thank you, sir. Thank you very much." Chidima's dad shook the man's hand and took the business card. The man led them outside to an empty stall area.

"Try selling your coffee for an hour and let me know how it goes."

"Of course. Thank you again," her dad said.

Chidima and her dad began to fill paper cups with the coffee. One person came and took a sip. That person told another person and before they knew it a small crowd had gathered around their stand. Chidima was so excited to see that not only was the coffee popular back home in Nigeria but it was just as popular here in America. It seemed like life might start getting pretty busy for her family. And that thought made her smile.

Assonance and Alliteration

Ailynn Collins mentored Caroline Strickland through a revision focused on the sound of words—specifically assonance and alliteration—in her poem, *Flames*.

Dear Reader,

When writing a poem, we have to think about what we're trying to get across to our readers.

Caroline had a wonderful experience at a campfire one night. She wanted to share her feelings about the fire in her poem. As she wrote her thoughts down, she had to decide which words would do the best job of conveying what she felt to her readers. She thought about the sounds a fire makes and the feelings it inspired in her. She found words that sounded like a crackling fire, to bring across what she wanted to express.

In our revision, we looked at *assonance in poetry*. Assonance is a literary term that refers to the repetition of a vowel sound in a line or stanza of poetry.

In *Flames*, assonance is seen in phrases like "with it's swirly twirly flames," where the 'ir' sound is repeated to make the reader feel as if the fire is dancing before their eyes. There are also lots of long 'a' sounds in 'haze', 'blaze', 'wane'. These long, sleepy sounds reflect how Caroline felt when she watched the fire burn.

As we looked over her poem for assonance, we kept in mind the sound of the words that were chosen. We thought of their assonant qualities—the open vowel sounds like the long 'ay' and 'ie' give the poem a dreamy feel, a lazy (in a good way) feel of sitting around a fire and getting sleepy. This contrasts with the short 'a' sounds that reflect the pop and crackle of the fire snapping the wood. These sounds might make another person sit up and be more alert.

These two contrasting feelings in the poem are brought out in the words chosen for this poem. Readers will bring their own experiences to the reading of the poem, guided by the sounds that the words make.

When you write a poem, think about the sounds that the words make. How do they bring out the feelings that we're trying to convey? Are they short and sharp, or long and easy? You might only need to change a word or two, much like Caroline did in her revision, but those changes could make all the difference.

Happy Writing,

Ailynn Collins

Ailynn Collins has been a Montessori teacher for many years, and loves sharing her love of books and writing with her students. She has an MFA in Writing for Children and Young Adults from Hamline University. She is the author of several books for young and middle grade readers– mainly science fiction and nonfiction stories. When she's not writing, she is working with her five dogs on agility, obedience, and rally competitions. She is excited to join Young Inklings and share her love for writing with young authors everywhere.

Caroline Strickland

Caroline is in fourth grade at the Athens Renaissance School near Huntsville, AL. In her spare time she likes to write, draw, and play with her brothers, Joseph and Thomas, and her dog, Willow. She enjoys her scout activities such as camping and sitting around a bonfire, having fun with her friends. When she grows up she hopes to be an author of some very good books. She'd like to illustrate them too.

Ailynn Collins: When did you start writing?

Caroline Strickland: I started writing when I was very young. I drew a lot of pictures and drew stories to go along with them. Once, I drew a picture of two hearts holding hands. One was my mom and one was me. I also put a blob in the corner. These were apparently zombies. I was four. My mom was mad with me because she loves me a lot, and she didn't like the idea of zombies eating us.

Q: How did it feel to revise your poem?

A: Revising was almost as fun as writing the poem. I got to choose better words and better phrases. I think it was really fun. I did it with my mom. She helped me along.

Q: Do you have advice for Young Inklings about revision?

A: I think my advice is don't spend to much time trying to get it to be perfect. Try to make your writing as good as you can make it. Try your best.

Q: Why do you enjoy writing?

A: I like the part where people get to enjoy reading my stories. When they're finished, the stories form a bigger picture than words on a page. I really like that feeling.

Q: Do you prefer poetry or prose?

A: I prefer writing stories, but I wrote this poem because we were writing poems at school. A couple of nights later we were at a campfire. That's what gave me the inspiration for the poem. My teacher said it didn't have to rhyme, so I put my thoughts onto paper.

Q: What sort of stories do you like to write?

A: I like fiction stories, like adventures of where normal people, someone like me, or even someone like a king or queen, goes on an adventure to find something that they need, to help themselves or others. These adventures would never happen in real life, but the stories usually start in a real life setting.

Q: How do you come up with your ideas?

A: I normally just hear or think of a name, then I start building a character. It takes me a while and I build it in my head. Or I play a game and think it would make a cool story. Then I'll build up the characters more. My brothers and I play a lot of games like that—role playing games. Sometimes I get my ideas from these games.

Q: Who do you enjoy sharing your stories with?

A: I don't enjoy sharing them with people outside of my family. I feel like I'd rather have my family's feedback than someone else's. I normally tell them my stories and ask what they like and what they would change.

Q: Are you working on a new story now?

A: I'm working on twenty-five! I have a bad habit of not finishing any of my stories. I have ten pages of a story and then I start a new story. I never come back to them. I haven't finished many of my stories.

Flames

by

Caroline Strickland

Flames
I love a good fire.
with its swirly twirly flames.
Above them
a slightly foggy haze
and the wonderful warmth
of the fiery hot blaze.
And the pop, pop, crack!
As the fire burns and logs snap,
this mesmerizing sound
makes me want to nap.
The pop, pop, crack!
of the embers blazing on.

People, young and old,
watch the graceful flame
dance around,
brave and bold,
tall in the high high sky,

like a burning orange pole.
As the flickering fire wanes,
the small haze
starts to fade
and the swirly twirly blaze
goes dormant once again.
Now I begin to tire,
and the flames are not higher
than they used to be.
But I still remember,
the fierce
and beautiful
fire.

Setting Details

Beth Spencewood advised Claire Reiger on a revision of *Smile for Me*, using setting details to make the world of the story real for her readers.

Dear Reader,

Writing an entire story through letters written by the characters can be tricky. How can the reader feel like they are watching the story unfold when the characters are never in the same room together? For this revision, Claire and I decided to focus on including setting details to bring the reader into the places mentioned in the story.

For inspiration, we discussed ideas like carrying a notebook and jotting down unique setting details that Claire saw in her own life that stood out to her. Another strategy was to find similar settings to the ones in her story and writing down as many descriptive details as possible about those places. Claire also sketched the places in her story to help her visualize these settings. We also talked about incorporating all five senses when possible, so the reader could not just see a place in their mind but feel it, touch it, taste it, and hear it. Then, Claire thought about which of the setting details would stand out to these particular characters and would be something they would want to share with each other in their letters. By adding these details, Claire invited the reader into the places her characters are sharing with each other.

While this process is particularly helpful when a story doesn't happen in scene like this one, a writer could use these strategies to add richness to any setting in their work. Give it a try in your own writing! See how adding a few specific setting details can bring the places in your writing to life.

Happy revising!

Beth Spencewood

Beth Spencewood grew up in Minneapolis, Minnesota where she spent the long winters reading her favorite books and writing funny stories starring her friends. She has an MFA in writing and writes novels for young adults. When she isn't writing she's reading, traveling, playing board games, learning a new craft, or exploring her neighborhood with her family.

Claire Reiger

Claire Reiger is an eighth grader in Redmond, Washington. She writes in different genres, but especially loves to write sad stories set in the 1800s. Her other interests included playing video games with her family, coding, reading fantasy novels, and watching her favorite shows and movies. Claire is thankful she was given the opportunity to participate in the Young Inklings contest.

Beth Spencewood: When did you start writing?
Claire Reiger: In fourth grade. I mainly wrote fantasy stories.

Q: What changed in *Smile for Me* when you started to think about the setting details?
A: What changed is how I visualized what I was writing. I paid more attention to what I saw in my head and transferred those images into words so the reader could see what I saw. The revision improved my story by adding more depth and made the world seem more real.

Q: What made you decide to write this story as letters back and forth between the characters?
A: I thought it would be a nice challenge for me. I've never done anything like this so I thought it could be fun. I thought it would be an interesting perspective.

Q: What is it about the 1800s that makes you like to write about that time period?
A: I think that the concept of people being willing to pack up their entire lives to move and not knowing how hard it's going to be but knowing it won't be easy. It was a different time, but it almost was like a whole different world.

Q: What advice do you have for other young authors who might not like to revise?
A: Revising is a necessary part of the process and it's always good to do with another person who can give you feedback and who you can talk to about it. It makes it more enjoyable, especially if it's someone you like to be around.

Q: How do you come up with new ideas for stories?
A: I think about music I listen to. The lyrics or melodies help me think of new ideas.

Q: Do you ever feel blocked? If so, what do you do to get unstuck?
A: I definitely do feel like sometimes it is hard to get words on the paper. Sometimes I'll take a break from that story to get my mind off it, and come back to it later. Taking a step back gives you a new way to look at your story, especially if you've been staring at it for who knows how long.

Q: Are you writing anything new?
A: I am writing something new at the moment. It is (surprise!) another 1800s story. It has six main characters so it's new to have to keep track of all that. I want it to be a bit longer. After that, I might take a break from writing about the 1800s and write something else.

Smile for Me

by

Claire Reiger

January 29, 1848

My Dearest Marie,

    I have wonderful news, my love. Today I finally turned in the paperwork for the house! I got the key and the place is officially ours. It's a lovely little cottage on a hill overlooking a large field of tall grass and wild flowers. It was a long time coming but the extra money I have been making off my sketches and the money you have been sending me from the bakery has really helped. It won't be long now until you and your family can move up here to Washington. I still haven't found a good location for your grandmother's bakery, one that is within our price range anyway.

It feels like I'll have to wait a million years to see you again. I still can't believe the last time I saw you was seven months ago, when I first left Oregon. I never stop thinking about you and the marvelous life we will have soon. It will only take a little more time.

With all my love,
William

February 5, 1848

My Dearest William,

I can't wait to see you again! Good job on getting the house deal finished. I know you are really working hard for this. Things are still going good back here. Grandmother taught me how to make her special pecan pie this morning. I burnt mine, but she says I just need a little more practice. Judging by the blackened crust and the smoke coming off it, I need much more than a little.

I started a garden behind the house that I have been tending to for a few days now. I've been growing cherry tomatoes, corn and watermelons. It's an odd combination of fruits and vegetables, but they are all Grandmother's favorites! I know I will have to let it go in a few months, but it will be nice for the next family who buys the house. Our bakery is still doing quite well, and with all the travelers passing through we get even more business. I wish I could work full time at the bakery to help Grandmother, but someone must take care of the farm animals. Oh! I almost forgot. My horse, Fiona, gave birth to a healthy female foal just yesterday. We still haven't thought of a name yet, so if you have any ideas please tell me! You always did have a close bond with Fiona. Do you remember when we would ride her every evening after school when we were, I think, six. And you nearly fell off her back into that mud puddle the first time you rode her. We laughed and laughed until our stomachs hurt. We should go on a ride through the fields when we get to Washington. It would be fun to do that again with you.

With all the love in the world,
Your soon to be wife,
Marie

February 12, 1848

My Dearest Marie,

I was thinking all week about names for the foal. What about the name Diana? It's a beautiful name for a new baby. And seeing as you slyly brought up embarrassing stories, you surely remember the first time I took you boating on Lake Maria. I had thought it was the perfect idea. The lake had been sprinkled with water lilies in full bloom, the water was clear to the bottom so you could see the schools of small fish swimming by, and the lake wasn't deep, so I thought there was nothing to fear. I was sure that

it was a beautiful and romantic place to be. But every time a lone fish swam by you would freeze up and forget to paddle. Then heavens forbid a school of fish swam by as you were reaching out to touch the calm surface of the water. You started squawking and flailing your paddle around that it's a miracle we didn't go over. I'm just teasing you, love. I know it was scary for you then but at least now we can smile at that memory.

I finally found a great building for the bakery. It's not too expensive and it is near the town square so there will be lots of customers. I sent you some sketches I drew of the place with the letter. I think you will both really like it. I have a big project coming up for work. The boss assigned us a lot to do, but I think this is my chance for a promotion. I should get a head start on working before tomorrow's shift.

With all the love the stars can hold,
William S.

February 19, 1848

My Dearest William,

I received the sketches of the bakery you sent me. They are gorgeous! The soft colors, the detail, and the perfection in each brush stroke. I love the little place you have picked out. The big windows

44

make the place feel welcoming and flower boxes under them gives the place life. Planting tulips in the flower boxes would make the place feel as calm as hillside in the summer when the wind blesses the land with a cool breeze. I showed the bakery painting to Grandmother and she loved it as well. She only talks of going there and of making you a cinnamon roll for finding that place. Speaking of sweet things, Fiona's little baby Diana is the nicest little horse ever. She is always happy and never bites, which makes parenting easier for Fiona.

On a much more serious note, Grandmother woke up not feeling well a few days ago. She has gotten a little worse since then and hasn't been able to work at the bakery. I have been working overtime to cover her shift and keep the house and farm in order. She says it's not bad enough to see a doctor for, but I don't agree. She shivers constantly, no matter the number of blankets she has, and she is still running a fever. I thought you should know. I will let you get back to your work now. I love you.

In your arms soon,
Marie

February 26, 1848

My Dearest Marie,

Love, I am terribly sorry to hear about your Grandma. But she is a strong-willed woman, and I believe she can overcome this.

No matter how stormy the clouds get, there is always a sun in the sky behind them. And if she says she will be okay, then you can trust her. Just keep an eye out for signs it is worsening. Make sure to keep yourself healthy too. Working overtime is not good. Trust me I know. I have been working long hours every night until the sun sinks away and past then, only to work the next day. Only the thought of you keeps me going. Maybe you could take a day of the week off to unwind and relax? It might keep your stamina full. I unfortunately must get back to work now. If anything goes south, please write and let me know.

With my love and protection,
William

March 10, 1848

My Dearest William,

  Grandmother is still not well. She is sleeps constantly and has no strength to do much of anything. Whenever she is awake, though, she is smiling. The sickness seems to have not fazed her. I can't help but wonder if she is doing that so I don't worry. Nevertheless, a doctor is scheduled to come in three days. I pray it is nothing bad. I must head to work now so I can be there for the early breakfast.

Sent with the smile of the sun,
Marie

March 17, 1848

My Dearest Marie,

For some good news, I got promoted two days ago! I worked hard on our last project. I am doing double the work any other writer does, and it paid off! My pay was increased, and I get to start working my way up in the company. The house is also looking much better. I repainted it to be a soft blue like you said you have always wanted, and I replaced the damaged boards in the fence. Tomorrow I'm going to tackle the broken pantry door which refuses to shut fully. I promise you by the heavens our life in Providence will be wonderful. As soon you arrive here, we will go riding through the fields like we used to as children.

I also wanted to mention something I noticed with your last letter. Your handwriting was very shaky. You have already overworked yourself. Your body and mind can't take so much stress all at once, and your Grandma being ill does nothing but add to that stress. Please take my advice and start taking a day or two off to relax each week. Do something to help yourself. I can work to make up the extra money by selling paintings on the side. It will be okay. I would hate to see you burn yourself out.

Stay beautiful my love,
William

March 29, 1848

My Dearest Marie,

Are you all right? I haven't gotten a letter from you and I'm worried sick. Please write to me as soon as you can. If something happened terrible happened, I need to know no matter what it is. I want to be here for you even if I'm not by your side. And if you need me to, I will gladly get home to you as fast as I can. Please write to me when you have the time.

I love you,
William

March 31, 1848

My Dearest William,

I am so sorry I couldn't write to you sooner. I rode with Grandma all night long to get to a better hospital two towns over in Shellsville. Her condition is bad. The doctor that came said there wasn't much he could do but said a doctor friend of his might be able to help. He rode with us to make sure we got to the hospital as quickly as possible. I don't know the condition she is in yet. I just know it isn't good. I'm sorry this letter is so short. I have a lot on my mind from working so much and from Grandmother being sick. I'm going to take your advice and try to relax. I think I am going to do some reading.

Sending my Love,
Marie

April 6, 1848

My Dearest Marie,

I am sorry to hear your grandma has fallen more ill. There is still hope for her so don't lose faith now. A new project is coming in, so I must get started on another long week. This project is smaller than the last but still a lot of work. This one should give me almost enough to buy the bakery. I already had quite a bit saved up. I hope your grandma will be happy to hear this. Please rest up and don't overwork yourself again and tell her I hope she gets well soon.

Sending my love and prayers,
William

April 14, 1848

My Dearest William,

You are working so hard. I am proud of you and to be your fiancé. Just remember to take a break once and a while too. Overworking yourself will do you no good, as you said yourself. Grandmother seems to be doing better now. She is staying awake for longer and can sit up in bed. I also think you should wait a bit more to buy the bakery. Grandmother will need more time to fully recover and getting the house in better shape to live in is more important. You always said you felt uncomfortable in an empty house because there was no personality or life in it. You wouldn't even look at the old abandoned house that used to sit down the road. You would squirm every time we rode past it. Or

when the first time you came over to my house after we had moved, you brought a paintbrush with you because I had told you the shed was unpainted. You had said that you couldn't stand by as our house was cursed with ugly, grey sheets of plaster that are not covered by gentle layers of beauty. You always had a way with words. I love you, William. Never forget that.

Your love is worth more to me than time itself,
Marie

April 28, 1848

My Dearest Marie,

If I wait for the bakery it might be sold to someone else, but if you truly think we should wait then I understand. The wellbeing of your Grandma is more important. I can always look for another bakery if it is sold.

On a different topic, I am sorry that my letters have been dreadfully short recently. I wish I had more time to write but my work gets in the way. The projects I get assigned are always more difficult than they seem. But I promise to make it up to you. When you head out on the wagon, when your Grandma is well of course, then I will ride as fast I as can to meet you so we can make the journey together. This will all work out in the end.

Stay strong and beautiful,
William

May 8, 1848

My Dearest Marie,

    My love I have not yet received your letter. It is likely a delay in with the postal service, but I wanted to write to make sure you and you Grandmother are all right. If anything is the matter than please tell me. I want nothing more than to help you if something is wrong so I can see you smile again. I am finishing up my work project so I will be able to write you longer letters soon.

Please take care and write me when you can,
William

May 16, 1848

My Dearest Marie,

    Please Marie, are you all right? I have had no word from you for weeks. If anything happened to you or your Grandma, please tell me. You can't leave me in the dark like this. I promised to be there for you, and I would do anything to help you. If I don't get word soon, I'll ride to Oregon to make sure you are safe myself. Even if it costs me my job. Just please write to me, it kills me to not know if you are okay.

I love you,
William

Dear William S,

This is Marie's grandmother, Minnie. It is with my deepest sorrow that I must write to you and be the one to explain the full truth, and to inform you neither me nor my granddaughter will be joining you in Providence. Please do not waste your money and time on getting the bakery. You should spend it on building your future. It's what Marie had wanted. But my dearest Marie is not able tell you herself because on May 11th, Marie passed away. It was a peaceful death, I promise you. She went in her sleep as I held her hand. She didn't tell you when she first became sick because she thought it would pass quickly. When it worsened dramatically, she couldn't tell you she was ill out of fear that you would lose everything you had. I didn't agree with this right away, but her tears changed my heart. If you were to know she was sick, you would have been a good husband and rushed to her side. Costing you your job, lots of money, time, and opportunity. If you lost her, she wouldn't want you to lose even more, to be trapped in a void with nothing but loss and misery around you, she had told me. But she never lied. She never, never told you a lie.

When I had gotten sick, she quickly picked up all house work and started full time shifts at the bakery by herself, just to support me. She would wake at five before the sun came and go to work at the bakery. I wouldn't see her until ten in the evening when all the chores were done. But she too soon fell ill. Still, she kept trying to work. But I could see the pain on her face as she rose for work each morning. And I didn't want that for her, she had already suffered so much with the death of her mother and father. I couldn't sit by. Seeing her handwriting to you was the kick in the back. As you saw it had been so shaking and scratchy. I called a doctor. He couldn't help us himself, but he knew a doctor friend who might have been able to. We rode all night in the back of his wagon, racing to the hospital. She cried all the way there thinking of how worried you must be. She hadn't had the strength to write to you in a while. It had hurt too much.

We got help in the hospital, and I started to recover. Marie, however, kept getting worse. With every passing day you could see the color drain from her face, her voice beginning to crack, and her body weakening. She became so weak she was unable to write to you. But every day she smiled as I read her the letter that had just come from you. She talked so much about you in her final days. Always telling anyone who would listen about something you had said or done or drawn. Marie even kept every letter and sketch you ever gave her in a little wooden box. You could walk into her room at any time, day or night, and if she was awake then she would be re-reading your letters. She would look up, a big smile on her face, and ask if you wanted to hear a story.

She really loved you, William, with all her heart. She had told me before she went that if she never recovered, that if she died in that hospital, that as long as you found happiness again in your life when she was gone, it would be all right. She would always be with you, congratulating you when you re-marry, cheering you on with every promotion, smiling with you every step of the way. I hope you know there is no force on Earth that would make Marie truly gone. So, when you get ready to sleep and hear the wind blow in sweet little notes through the window, know that was Marie, wishing you good night, and a wonderful life.

Please take care,
Minnie R.

Rhythm

Dear Reader,

Poems are great places to practice rhyme and word choice to explore rhythm. When I met with Chris to revise his poem, *I AM GREAT*, we decided to play with rhythm to see how that would add to his already powerful poem.

Chris did a fantastic job writing a poem that is inspirational. He did a great job of using rhyme to make the point of confidence land for a reader. Chris has a great gift in creating words that flow together to create a rhythm. We first discussed how rhythm is how a poem flows and beats, and how it sounds. With a few key changes we were able to strengthen the message and rhythm of the piece.

In his revision, Chris focused on two main points to impact the rhythm. First, Chris identified key words that were most important. We worked together to figure out different tools, like punctuation and bold text, to make these words stand out. We looked at specificity and creating examples that were realistic based in Chris's current life and experiences. These examples helped make the poem flow closer to Chris' unique voice. Next, we worked on structure. Chris had a strong pattern of five line stanza sections in his piece. We worked on making this pattern more uniform in the piece to help keep the rhythm he created. By adding a single line or word we were able to add rhythm and strength to the piece.

If you are writing a poem, you might want to try Chris' approach. Pick out sections and find the pattern of the piece. Choose places that the pattern changes and know what will stick out! Know a little change goes a long way when playing with rhythm.

Cheers!
Philomena Block

Philomena Block is an actor, writer, and comedian originally from Santa Cruz, California. Philomena holds two bachelor's degrees—one in musical theatre, the other in psychology—and is trained in playwriting, sketch comedy, and improvisation. Philomena has always been drawn to storytelling and loves developing characters onstage and on the page. Philomena worked as a teacher with Society of Young Inklings for two years and is so happy to keep supporting young writers with the Inklings Book Contest. When Philomena isn't writing or performing, she works as a marketing professional and loves breathing in the ocean air.

Chris L. Matthews, II

Chris L. Matthews, II (aka C.J.) is a seventh grader in Atlanta, GA. He enjoys the arts, playing video games, and helping others. He has always liked to read and write and hopes to one day publish a book of his own. He practices mindfulness, which he learned from one of his mentors, author and former NFL running back, Prince Daniels, Jr. Since he was only 5 years old he has organized an annual blanket collection for kids who need an extra dose of comfort. His family is very proud of him, but what he is most proud of is being big brother to three-year-old, Kollin.

Philomena Block: Why do you like to write?
Chris Matthews: I like to write because it's another way to express yourself. And you can always revise. Even if you put your foot in your mouth, you can always edit. You can change almost anything.

Q: Where do you usually like to write and with what?
A: I like to write in a quiet place, but not completely silent. I prefer typing my writing out because if you don't like to mess up, it's already ready to edit. It makes it so you can't mess up.

Q: What do you want other kids to get or learn from your poem?
A: I want other kids to know that you can be anything you want. If you put in hard work and effort and try. I want kids to feel inspired when they read my poem. I don't want them to feel like they can't, BECAUSE THEY CAN!

Q: What changed when you revised your poem?
A: The rhythm changed and a lot of the mood. Some of the small words were changed to big words, and that changed how you feel when you read it.

Q: How did you feel after first revising your poem and editing for rhythm? Any favorite changes?
A: It wasn't as hard as I thought, but it also wasn't easy. My favorite change was adding the lessons my parents taught me to the poem and making that more specific.

Q: In addition to your writing, you've worked on some very meaningful projects. Tell us about Blankies 4 My Buddies.
A: When I was five, my family experienced a pregnancy loss and I struggled with losing my unborn sister, Karsen Angelica. Seeking comfort for me, my mother asked me, "If you could help other kids, what would you do?" I explained that I never wanted any child to feel loneliness, a feeling that frequented my heart when the baby did not come home. My mother set up a GoFundMe campaign and asked friends and family members across the country to donate money for my cause. We created Blankies 4 My Buddies, and for six years now, I've been collecting warm blankets to provide an extra dose of comfort to kids who are sick or displaced.

Q: How has the project been going?
A: Great! In March, I was recognized as the Community Service honoree at the 2019 YOU Awards. In 2017, I was a recipient of a Disney Summer of Service grant and my family used the grant to launch the First Annual Giving Bowl, a 7-on-7 charitable flag football game to

feed families and collect blankets for residents in my South Atlanta community for the holidays. This November, our family will host the third annual event. With the help of community partners, we've been able to feed in excess of fifty families each year.

Q: Do you use your writing to help with your cause?
A: Yes! In fact, I've already completed writing a children's book to share the story of my family's loss to empower kids with the same experience. My mom is helping me to have the book illustrated and hopefully published.

Q: Do you have any advice for the young writers of America?
A: Always do your best. You have to put in the work, but it's worth it!

I AM GREAT!

by

Chris L. Matthews, II

I AM GREAT

(a message to young kings and queens everywhere)

One day I will be great.
Actually, I already am!
But when I'm a man …
more people will understand.
MY PURPOSE.

My parents are always teaching me lessons.
Work hard. Be Kind. Be a leader. Treat people the way you want to be treated.
They say that I am a blessing…
to them and to others.
Both me and my little brother.

They call us young kings
Because we can do anything.
If we just try…
Our limit is the sky.

Famous people have paved the way for me.
Barry Sanders. Nick Cannon. Barack Obama.
For us!
We no longer have to sit at the back of the bus…

One day I CAN BE THE PRESIDENT!
But for my parents…
that was never a goal.
Tides have changed now
and I have the WHOLE
World ahead of me.

I am handsome, creative, athletic, and smart.
I love helping people…
I have a really BIG heart.

With these tools,
There are no rules.
I have everything I need.
To SUCCEED.

I am working toward my future
And it looks really **BRIGHT**.
The closer and closer I move
I FIGHT
to prove…
to the world that I AM GREAT!

It's never TOO LATE or TOO SOON
To shoot for the moon.
Don't ever stop!
Keep going till you reach the top.

I AM GREAT!
You WILL SEE!
I can be anything that I want to be.
BUT IT STARTS WITH ME!

Building Tension

Gwen Lee helped Ching Yi Mak see how building tension came from adding conflict in her story, *The Ocean's Wrath*.

Dear Reader,

How do you build tension throughout a story so that it sustains the reader's interest right till the end? In *The Ocean's Wrath*, Ching Yi did a great job creating a sense of foreboding in the run up to the tsunami. In our revision, I wanted to see if we could heighten the anxiety the characters felt as they traversed the pre- and post-tsunami landscape by making some tweaks.

Ching Yi had started the story with a prologue in her original draft. Although the prologue was well written and set the overall mood well, it invariably gave away a twist in the story. During our revision, we examined the role of the prologue and whether it contributed to increasing or decreasing the overall sense of shock and surprise. Here are the two questions we asked ourselves in our brainstorming session. One, are you giving away something in the prologue that might have greater impact if revealed later in the story? Two, is there information in the prologue that can't fit elsewhere in the book? If not, do you have a good reason for not placing that information within the story proper?

Tension results not just from a person's reaction to the events unfolding (in this case, a tsunami), but also from the conflicts occurring between the different personalities. Often, when a piece of writing is too quiet, it is because there isn't enough conflict. I suggested to Ching Yi that she create different motivations for the various characters in order to bump up the interpersonal conflict.

If you find yourself struggling with a plot that feels too flat, try the above techniques to see if it makes a difference.

Happy writing!

Gwen Lee

Trained as an architect, Gwen Lee is the author of several children's books. Her first book *Little Cloud Wants Snow* has been translated to Korean and Mandarin, and is being used by schools in Texas, USA, to educate children about weather science. Today, Gwen is one of the few interdisciplinary writers straddling the fields of architecture and literature, writing for both children and adults alike. As a writing mentor with the Society of Young Inklings, she enjoys helping other writers develop their unique voices.

Ching Yi Mak

At the point of the competition, Ching Yi was a fourth grader in Pittsburgh, Pennsylvania. She has since returned to her home country, Singapore. Ching Yi likes to write and read. In addition, she loves to draw manga. She counts the fantasy writers Brandon Sanderson and Shannon Messenger and the manga artist Mark Crilley among her heroes.

Gwen Lee: Why did you decide to remove the prologue?
Ching Yi Mak: I decided to remove the prologue because it made sense not to give spoilers so early in the story, and there was no point inserting a prologue simply for the sake of having one.

Q: How do you think the story changed after the revision?
A: I corrected a great deal of logic gaps in the characters' actions, which definitely made the story a lot more realistic and believable.

Q: What advice do you have for other Young Inklings who don't like revision very much?
A: I think that revision truly improves your writing a lot, and it helps you see the flaws in your writing. So, unpleasant as revision may be, it is extremely important.

Q: Why do you enjoy writing?

A: I enjoy writing because I love reading, and I want to write like professional authors do. I also enjoy writing because I like the way you can express things in great detail, especially thoughts and emotions.

Q: What are your favorite books?

A: *The Reckoners* series by Brandon Sanderson, the *Sky Fall* series by Shannon Messenger, and the *Snow Like Ashes* series by Sara Raasch.

The Ocean's Wrath

by

Ching Yi Mak

CHAPTER I

I sat up in bed and listened to the gentle lapping of the waves against the shore. The dawn was still and calm, as if the whole world were asleep. Not even a bird dared punctuate the silence with its calls.

Drawing my knees to my chest, I leaned towards the window and rested my cheek against the glass, staring out across the open ocean through the hazy morning mist. In the distance, if I looked carefully, I could see streaks of yellow and red lighting up the gray sky. And I wondered, not for the first time, what was out there, beyond the churning waters. Beyond the life I knew.

I sat like that for a while, curling up under the blankets, looking out. Then, at last, I sighed, stood up, and walked outside.

Ellen was already there, sitting in the sand with her hands clasped. How tiny she looked, I thought, with the endless expanse of

blue in front of her. So small and vulnerable.

She looked up when I joined her. "Something is going to happen," she whispered, looking up at me with large, frightened eyes. "Something big. I know it."

I nodded but did not speak. I could feel it too, around me and inside me.

As if on cue, the earth rumbled slightly.

"It's all right, Ellen," I murmured to her, running my fingers through her hair.

She clung to me still, unwilling to let go. The house door opened and slammed shut behind us.

"Ellen. Peter," Father said sharply. "Get in the car. Quickly!" His voice was laced with panic, and I could practically see the fear radiating off him.

Ellen looked at me questioningly. I grabbed her hand and pulled her towards the car.

Father jumped into the car and started the engine.

"Wait!" Ellen said, lunging forward. "What about Mother?"

Father stepped out of the car, and I could see the grief in his eyes. "I don't know where she is," he said. "She went out this morning to walk the dog. There's no time to look for her."

Ellen went into the car first. I wanted to protest, to do something, but I knew what he meant. Worst of all, I knew he was right.

But even then, even as everything circulated through my head, my brain still worked, grasping desperately at anything I could find, anything that would cause the change I needed in Father's perspective.

I stood my ground. "I'm waiting for her."

Father put his hands on my shoulders. "No," he said sharply, wiping the tears from his eyes, and for a fraction of a second, I saw his mental shields go down.

All my life, he'd never shown a hint of emotion, but now, everything was laid bare before me. I looked into his eyes and found a tangled mess of feelings: Fear. Anger. Worry. Pain. Sadness. And, most of all, guilt.

Guilt for not preparing for this earlier. And guilt for not being a better parent.

And then, as quickly as it had started, his face had returned to being unreadable, and everything I had seen in him had been buried deep, deep down.

"We can't wait," he said, his face hard and impassive as he hauled me back towards the car, but I could still feel the world of emotions behind those four words.

Even then, it was reason against love, and we both knew which would win. But before I could move, Father threw me into the car beside Ellen, set the child lock on, and drove off.

CHAPTER II

As we navigated the streets, I realized how completely devoid of people our neighborhood was. Everyone was either evacuating or cowering in their homes, afraid to leave all they had lived for behind.

Ellen grabbed my hand, whimpering softly, and pointed behind us. I spun around in my seat and gasped.

The water was drawing back, leaving only a blank expanse of

wet sand behind it. I tensed. We didn't have much time before the tsunami struck.

Father turned back as well and began to accelerate. He understood the stakes better than anyone. I could tell that, for once, he was worried.

Ellen shook in my arms, her eyes wide with fear. I held her close, my eyes squeezed shut, trying not to envision all that could go wrong. My heart pounded in my chest, drumming a frantic rhythm that only seemed to accentuate my panic.

We were well away from the coast by now, and yet I knew without doubt that the tsunami would have no trouble reaching us, far away though we were.

As it turned out, I was right.

Water rushed forward, filling streets and buildings and anything in between. In an instant, we were submerged.

I began to panic. Water was all around me, swirling and pushing. I couldn't breathe, couldn't think. The car spun wildly, disorienting me, until up became down and right was left.

My lungs began to burn. There were only a few precious seconds left, and I clung to them like a lifeline, knowing that they were all I had. I could practically see death's cold fingers grasping for me, pulling me lower and lower…

Darkness encroached at the corners of my vision, unconsciousness threatening to overwhelm me. The cold stung me, numbing me from head to toe, and in pure desperation, I threw myself against the car door. It burst open, and I flung myself upwards.

Suddenly, a thought struck me, like a punch to the gut. Where was Ellen?

I swam back down, fear clouding my vision and bringing tears to my eyes. What if she was dead?

I felt for her hand in the perpetual gloom of the water. She had been sitting beside me a moment before…

There! I grabbed her and towed her upwards, fueled by adrenaline and panic alone. Father surfaced behind me, coughing hard.

I hauled myself–and Ellen–up onto a windowsill and propped her up against the glass, then felt for her pulse.

Please let her not be dead, I pleaded silently. *Please.*

The seconds passed, and it was agony to sit there, simply waiting, and hoping, knowing that there was nothing I could do.

And then, at last, Ellen coughed up water, and I sighed with relief. She was alive. Unconscious, perhaps, but she was alive.

A figure clambered weakly onto the ledge beside me. Father. I shied backwards, stunned by the sight that greeted my eyes.

"Peter," he said, choking out blood. "Leave me. Take Ellen and go."

I stared in disbelief at the piece of wood impaled in his chest . "No! I cried out, lunging forward. "No! Not now! Not after everything! We could get you to a doctor…and…"

Father shook his head, looking down at the blood streaming from his wound. "It's too late," he rasped.

I wanted to laugh, but the sound died in my throat. Because surely he was joking. He couldn't possibly be dying…could he?

"But–" I protested.

Father cut me off. "I'm just as good as dead, Peter. And there's no use saving a doomed man." His gaze met mine for the last time. "Take Ellen and go. The rescue camp shouldn't be far…" He slumped forward, his eyes glassy and unfocused, and I knew that he was gone.

Father was never coming back.

CHAPTER III

I trudged forward, keeping my eyes on the ground. Making sure I never looked up. The debris was all the same now, just broken doorways and cracked, collapsing buildings. And each time I saw a structure I recognized, a new pang of pain shot through my heart. It was easier to just stare at the murky waters swirling around my feet and keep stumbling along, one slow step at a time.

I shifted my grip on Ellen, finally raising my gaze forward. Nothing had changed from the streets before, and yet something was different.

There were people here now, I realized, milling about amidst the wreckage, scaling broken walls, climbing stairwells, tending to the injured… I hurried onward, and Ellen groaned in my grip, slipping in and out of consciousness.

As I advanced, it became clear that this was the rescue camp Father had been talking about. The wounded lay on makeshift beds, doctors rushing to each in turn, bandaging gashes and bruises. I paused, staring at each one in turn, and I imagined Father, limp and lifeless on the window ledge, blood still coating his chest, lying alone in the debris.

I forced the image away. I couldn't afford to be weak now, not with Ellen depending on me. She was all I had.

That thought echoed in my head as I pushed on. *She is all I have.* Mother was left behind, presumably dead, and Father was gone. *Gone forever.*

My knees began to shake but I kept walking, one foot after the other. I was alone now, alone in an entirely new world, with nothing but Ellen.

The tears came next, and though I held them back, the thoughts pounded at my head, over and over, until my mind was nothing but a haze of hopelessness and anxiety. Yet even then, they battered me, time after time, never slackening their grip, never ceasing.

You're on your own now. There's no one out there, no one who cares. Everyone's gone.

I squeezed my eyes shut, but those words came at me once again, repeatedly, relentlessly: *You're alone.*

CHAPTER IV

I held my breath, waiting as the wall of water roared forward, reaching for me, wanting to add my life to the many others it had claimed. And yet, I didn't feel anything but serenity. The calm before the storm. Closer and closer it came, nearer and nearer still…

"Peter!" someone yelled. "Peter!"

I jolted awake, started by the sudden bustle of activity around me.

"Peter!" Ellen said, tugging on my arm. "Come on!"

"Is something wrong?" I asked, jumping to my feet. And then I looked behind her.

A figure came barreling from the shadows towards us, and before I knew it, Mother was there, no different than when I'd last seen her. She hugged me, lifting me up into the air. She reminded me of home, and for a moment, it seemed that nothing had changed, that everything was back to normal.

Then Ellen asked one of the most important questions of all. "How did you survive?"

Mother smiled slightly, and told the story of her being stranded on the top floor of our home, looking out upon the destruction the tsunami had unleashed. From high up in the sky, she'd seen everything; all the pain and sadness that Ellen and I had only caught a glimpse. She sounded just like Father then, logical and resourceful. For a moment, I could almost believe that everything was back to normal again.

But no, not everything was the same. Because Father wasn't here.

And suddenly, the air was laced tight with tension as Mother asked, "Where's Father?" and everything collapsed into confusion and despair.

"He's gone," I whispered, so softly I didn't know how she could have heard me, and yet she squeezed me even tighter. "He's dead."

Then the tears came pouring out, burning my cheeks as Mother held me, never saying a word, but I knew, deep in my heart, that she felt the same way. Father had been our anchor, keeping us steady in the churning of the sea. But now the rope had broken, casting us adrift, our memories, the severed cord, reminding us of all we had lost.

Yet I thought of Mother, and of all I still had, and a sad smile crept across my face. Father was never coming back, but Mother was here, and Ellen. Life would still move on.

And so would I.

Word Choice and Tone

Jena McNealy mentored Carolina Ruiz through a revision that explored word choice to impact tone in her poem, *A Tribute To Shelter Animals*.

Dear Reader,

In a poem, there are very few words, and it is clear that Carolina chose each one carefully. In *A Tribute to Shelter Animals*, the tone of the poem changes with the description of two different pets. Carolina chose excellent words to create a specific tone for each point of view. In this revision, we chose to focus on word choice for tone. The last section of the poem is very powerful. Giving voice to the pets gives the reader a deeper understanding of their perspectives.

As you revise poetry think about how your word choice affects the tone and feeling of the poem. First, you want to ask yourself: What do I want a reader to feel after reading my poem?

The thing about poetry is that there is no right and wrong, so improving skill as a poet can be difficult.

The best revising tip I have for poets is to read the poem aloud or asking a friend to read it aloud. In Carolina's poem, lines that stood out to us the most were the lines with fewer words. Carolina swapped out different words and shortened a few lines. The small changes made the poem even better.

Enjoy!

Jena McNealy

Jena McNealy has always had a passion for education. She enjoys writing children's books and teaching preschool. Jena believes that all young learners deserve the opportunity to explore their creative potential. Jena holds a B.A in Creative Arts and a minor in Education from San Jose State University. In her spare time Jena enjoys traveling and cooking.

Carolina Ruiz

Carolina says, "I'm Carolina Ruiz and I'm a sixth grader. I enjoy writing, art, and theatre. I am particularly interested in animals. Cats are my favorite. I'm also inspired by nature. I hope you enjoy my poem."

Jena McNealy: When did you start writing?
Carolina Ruiz: I started writing at age three. I wrote about cats.

Q: Where do you like to write?
A: Wherever as long as I'm alone. I like to write in a quiet atmosphere so there's not a lot of distraction. The best ideas come to me at night. Unfortunately, sometimes I forget the ideas in the morning.

Q: Where did you get the idea for this poem?
A: It was inspired by another poem. It was also inspired by my own shelter cat.

Q: How do you feel about the revisions you made in *A Tribute to Shelter Animals*?
A: It was nice to go back and fix things that I wouldn't have fixed on my own.

Q: What advice do you have for other Young Inklings who don't like revision very much?
A: Don't try and write something you're not passionate about because you'll run out of ideas.

Q: Who do you share your writing with?
A: My friend, Marina.

Q: Are you working on anything new?
A: Yes I have a few pieces in the works. Also, I have one very long story that I write for fun.

A Tribute to Shelter Animals

by

Carolina Ruiz

A Tribute to Shelter Animals

I have two pets
And the first one
Is my dog named Rover
He is very loyal and by my side
Even when the day is over
I got him from a breeder

When he was just a puppy
And as he had been born to do
He has always loved me
He never bites or jumps or whines
Or chew up my clogs
He comes when called and sits when told
For he is a good dog

In his mind
He makes his worlds
Of beauty and of splendor
His imagination is bright and happy
And his heart and soul are tender
When Rover lays down to rest
And the morning's to be awaited
He jumps and plays and frolics
In the worlds he has created
Rover is my best friend
And I am his too

He runs and plays with me
And cheers me when I'm blue
If I cry
He sits by me
And licks my face all over
And that is why I love most
My beloved dog Rover

My second pet is my cat
And her name is Mitsy
She gives me bites and scratches
And hisses constantly
She tears open my sofa
And leaves my flower bed a mess
She can be a real pain
And causes me so much stress
At night she walks in darkness she's seen
And sees the hate she knows

For I got her from a shelter
When she was full grown
And the world once scratched and bit her
Pained her constantly
It tore her heart right open
Wrecked her soul and left debris
Her old master abused her
He kept her in a cage
Her ribs stuck out from hunger
And her fur was full of mange

One day they came and told him
That he couldn't keep her anymore
So not wanting to go to any trouble
He dumped her outside the door
She became a street cat
A life of hunger and neglect
Where people threw rocks and sticks at her
And starvation was a threat

They brought her to the shelter
But she was never the same
And there I found and adopted her
But on humans she had put the blame
Mitsy will never be my best friend
We both know full well that
She's cold and scarred from her life
And that's why I fear my cat

One night I dreamed
A little dream
Not at all real
But it seemed
That if my two pets
Could actually speak
They'd say what they had said
But for that, call me a freak
First came Rover, bounding up

And I patted him on the head
Then he opened his mouth to speak
And this is what he said
"Master, I know you love me
You have since I was a pup
I was bred specially
For when you fall down I pick you up
I want you to see each beautiful thing
I see in this world
For a shadow needs a light
As so I have been told
I see magic in my dreams
Each night I go to sleep
And Master, if you could only see it
Like me you'd play and leap
I'm always there when you are sad
I sit when I am told
I never bark or bite or jump

For I have a heart of gold
I am with you day and night
Rain or sun or fog
I know because you tell me
I am a good dog"
Then came Mitsy
She walked without a sound
She looked so solemn, her ears were hung

And her head turned to the ground

She didn't hiss or run away
Which for her was very strange
And all she simply said was:
"I'm sorry. I can change."

I awoke early in the morning
Before the sun had shown its head
Trusty Rover was on the floor below me
And Mitsy on my bed

Mitsy and I will never be best friends
But we'll try as long as we live
For as long as I try to understand
She will try to forgive

Building Tension with Setting

Melody Reed worked with Sanjay Ravishankar on creating tension through the setting of his suspenseful tale, *An Adventurous Story*.

Dear Reader,

Adventure stories need enough suspense to keep the reader captivated. *An Adventurous Journey*, by Sanjay Ravishankar, is a great example. His action-packed story, about the love of family, is filled with both external and internal conflicts. The reader is anxious to see what happens next.

We decided to focus on *Building Tension with Setting*. Sanjay has laid out increasingly difficult situations for the siblings, Raj and Dhana, and their dad, Ramu to navigate. Each difficulty the characters experienced could be expanded, to create further tension, by adding sensory details to the setting.

Try thinking about the locations in your favorite movie. We used scary movies as our focus. The director sets the scene in a dark forest. The trees are dead, and shadows seem to lurk between them. The only sound you hear is wolves howling in the background. You smell an odor you can't quite place, but it makes your nose crinkle in disgust. The eerie setting alone puts the reader on edge.

Sanjay and I identified places in his story where this technique would work. One location is where the siblings have to retrace their steps leading back to their dad. So many bad things have happened up to this point that the characters are wary. By adding light strokes of sensory details to the setting such as, "It was so quiet, he heard the crickets chirping," Sanjay was able to show the reader the intensity of the scene.

Next time you're watching a movie, pay attention to the details of the setting. See what immerses you in the story. Use that as a model for your writing.

Congratulations, Sanjay! Thank you for sharing your work.

Happy Writing,

Melody Reed

Melody Reed is a writer, teacher, and young adult library reference assistant who has far more books than her house can hold. As a writing mentor through Society of Young Inklings, she finds joy in sharing the knowledge she has learned from all the generous writers who have touched her life. Melody earned a bachelor's degree in Science from the University of St. Francis and an MFA in Writing for Children and Young Adults from Hamline University. When she is not working with young writers or young readers, she enjoys taking nature walks looking for inspiration. She is currently revising her YA novel, which includes a lot of science. She lives in Chicago with her family and two precious little dogs.

Sanjay Ravishankar

Sanjay is a sixth grader at Harvest Park Middle School. He has two pet dogs and loves reptiles. In his free time, he plays basketball with his dad and sister. He loves to read and write.

Melody Reed: Why do you like to write stories?
Sanjay Ravishankar: I like to write stories because writing shapes my imagination into words and I can share my ideas with everyone.

Q: How do you come up with your ideas?
A: Sometimes an idea just pops in my head and if it sounds good, I write it in my story.

Q: Where do you like to write?
A: I usually like to write at the kitchen counter or outside. I like to write, especially, in my backyard. It's a natural place and it gives me a lot of ideas.

Q: How did you come up with the idea for this particular story?
A: I was interested in animals and I kept on building the idea in my head. I asked more questions and I thought of good obstacles.

Q: How long did it take you to write the draft of this story?

A: It took me around a week or so to write the story.

Q: What advice do you have for other Young Inklings who don't like revisions very much?

A: I think you should be open to feedback, if you take it or not. Also, the revisions are coming from a professional, so you should listen to them carefully.

An Adventurous Journey...

by

Sanjay Ravishankar

6: 33 PM

As Raj shivered yet another spider off his back, he saw some smoke at a distance. Raj, his sister Dhana, and his dad, Ramu were all coming back from a successful day of woodcutting. Raj put out the tiny lantern in his hand. There was only a little oil left. Raj decided, *let's save it for some time when it is actually needed*. He swung it around his arm and tried to keep up with his sister and dad. As they neared their village, the smoke was heavy, and the visibility was poor.

Raj asked his dad suspiciously, "Does that smoke look normal to you?"

Ramu replied, "No, it doesn't, let's go check it out."

This same suspicion had been lingering in his mind for a long time. The thick scent of smoke wasn't usual. Even though he was a brave man, he was disturbed by the situation.

As they all sprinted towards the end of the jungle with fear, the

smoke got thicker. Ramu peered out of the jungle into their village. He couldn't believe his eyes. Most of the huts around were burnt down to the ground! Thankfully, theirs wasn't. There was fire everywhere.

Ramu's first parental instinct was, "Save the kids."

He motioned for them to stay back, and he rushed towards their house.

Ramu called to his wife, Lakshmi. "Lakshmi? Are you home?" he yelled. No response. "Hello..?" Still no response.

He was frightened about the safety of Lakshmi, and the pungent smell of smoke was not helping.

Ramu's pale face made Raj's stomach twist. The kids couldn't wait any longer. They ran towards their dad, anguished. Dhana doubled over, coughing. Raj's hand slowly crept and held Dhana's. The three of them searched everywhere, but Lakshmi wasn't to be seen. As they slowly mourned and shuffled around the village, they could see many burnt bodies of their neighbors.

Raj thought, "None of them looked like Mom's. Is that good or bad?"

All of a sudden, Dhana started crying uncontrollably. As Raj tried to comfort, Ramu reflected his experiences.

"It must have only been a mediocre fire, but it was sufficient enough to take down lives of many," he thought.

Ramu could see the efforts taken by the villagers to control it. But alas, a lot of people lost their lives. One side of him ached for his missing wife, but the other wanted to bring the kids to safety.

Ramu spoke, "Kids, it is not safe here. Let's move to Bagalkot, across the jungle."

8:02 PM

Under the bright moonlight, Raj was walking through the jungle with his dad and sister. Mostly, they were silent. Thoughts of Mom and the fire raced through his mind. He trudged through the crooked "path." He sighed as he remembered the past. They had lived in a peaceful village in Karnataka, India, near Jog Falls Environ Forest.

Jog Falls was known as the ninth most dangerous forest in the world, even though it had beautiful falls in the depths of it. Raj– ten years old–lived with his 7-year old sister Dhana and his parents, Ramu and Lakshmi.

Their main job was woodcutting, while Lakshmi made pottery at home. The villagers were nice and kind-hearted. During Raj's trips to the forest, his dad would teach him tricks and tips to survive in the wilderness. Oh, how he loved that life. Now, everything was ruined by the fire. Suddenly, he was snapped back to reality by his father's groans. He was lying on the ground.

Raj asked hurriedly, "What happened?"

Ramu didn't reply. Instead, he turned over. There, on his left knee, was a gold scaly snake.

Raj gasped, "A saw scaled viper."

His dad struggled for words. "It…bit me. Go find…Kapikachu seeds," his voice trailed off.

Raj felt nauseous, like he was going to faint. His mind was whirling. *First Mom, now Dad too? When will it ever end?* Raj thought to himself.

Dhana silently put a hand on Raj's shoulder.

Dhana said, "It's okay. Everything will be fine."

Raj wanted to scream, *"No, it's not!!!!"* But instead, he kept calm and forced a smile. "Come on, we have only ten hours."

The two siblings helped move their dad to a safer place. Then, they set out to save their dad.

11:21 PM

Even though they had been searching for a long time, nothing was found.

Dhana asked, "How long do we have left?"

Raj replied, glancing at the bright moon, "Around seven hours. A saw-scaled viper bite takes at the most ten hours for the venom to strike the heart."

Raj muttered to himself. "Why didn't Dad tell us where the seeds are?"

"Well, we do know what they look like. Remember that day when we found some? Dad said that they were very rare, and that they cure most snake bites."

"Remind me why we are in the deeper side again." Raj grumbled.

"Because it wasn't anywhere in the path we took to get here, so we decided to venture deeper. In fact, you're the one who bought up that idea."

After a few more horrible moments of uprooting each plant, Dhana felt as if there were eyes burning through her back.

She piped up, "Don't you have the feeling something is watching us?"

Raj replied, "No, why do you?"

He was cut short by an echoing growl behind them. They both turned around. From the bushes, emerged a tiger! Its fur gleamed orange and black from the moon's reflection. Its eyes glowed, and it licked its whiskers. Dhana started running but Raj couldn't move. He was petrified.

"Come on!" Dhana pulled.

Raj didn't budge, like he was transfixed into that spot. Suddenly, he came back to reality.

"Dhana, the lantern!"

"What about the lantern? There is a tiger chasing us and I don't care about the lantern!"

"Just give me the lantern!"

"You have it!"

Coming back to his senses, Raj stepped out of the safety of the tall trees, and into plain sight. The tiger was approaching, around a hundred meters away. Raj struck the lantern, but nothing happened. Eighty meters away…still no luck with the oil lamp. Fifty meters away… Raj struck another time, but still the same result. Forty meters away… Thirty meters away…Twenty meters away…

Dhana pulled on her brother, "Raj, get back. The tiger is coming."

Raj whispered back, "I got this. Just wait."

He tried one more time. A small flame lit up! Raj lifted the lantern at the right time, and swished it around. The tiger leaped back into the bushes, where it belonged. Its dim-lit eyes were shown through the thick leaves, irritated and annoyed, clearly disappointed it didn't have a midnight snack.

The kids had some time. They collected logs and hurriedly threw them in the path. Dhana pulled Raj and they ran into another path.

Raj explained, "Don't you remember that Dad told us tigers are scared of light?"

They moved forward examining each plant. Raj and Dhana came across a fork in the path.

Raj said, "I will go left, you go right."

They split up and Raj walked along the left path. He was about to put out the lantern, but he heard a scream. He raced along, arriving at Dhana.

He asked her, "Are you okay? What happened?"

Dhana didn't reply. Instead she pointed forward. In front, there was a large river, at least thirty feet wide, and five miles long.

Dhana asked, "Are you seeing what I am?"

Raj squinted to see, so he took out the oil lamp once again.

Dhana repeated, "Are you seeing what I am?"

The most exciting thing he could see was a rock with moss on it. Dhana pointed to the side. Raj gasped. He saw a bush of Kapikachu across the river!

"Come on, what are we waiting for?" he yelled.

But alas, they had no boat. Raj tried putting a foot in, but it never touched the bottom. He shuddered. It was the middle of the night, and it was starting to get cold.

Dhana interrupted his thoughts, "Well..."

Raj said to Dhana, "There is no hope!"

Dhana replied, "There is always a way."

This time, Dhana got an idea. She told Raj, "Grab some thick logs."

For the next half an hour, they gathered broken logs and arranged them one by one. Dhana then took some long vines and tied about five logs together.

"There, our raft is done!" Dhana exclaimed.

She sat on it, and Raj gave it a push. At the last second, he jumped on. It took them about ten minutes to reach the other side. When they were close, they were excited. But they celebrated too soon. All of a sudden, a dark yellow blob jumped out of the water and on to the raft.

Dhana's eyes went wide. "A bull frog!" she stammered.

It jumped on her. "Ahhhhhhhhhhhhh!" she screamed as she toppled into the water.

The raft tilted, and Raj also tumbled into the darkness of the murky water.

Oh no, Dhana! Sisters can be such a pain sometimes. Raj thought to himself.

He struggled to reach his sister. He grabbed her and swam towards the shore. He reached out to the wet dirt, but missed. His hopes were giving up until his foot hit a rock. He climbed on to the silt.

Safe at last! Raj thought.

He climbed over and shook Dhana. "Dhana, Dhana, wake up!"

Dhana suddenly sat up. "Where is the Kapikachu?" she asked.

They both walked over the bush. To their disappointment, it was just a patch of wild flowers.

Raj groaned, "All that trouble for nothing."

Dhana fell down crying. "Why don't we do something right?" she cried. "I am worried about Dad. What if we lose him, like we did

to Mom?"

She tried her best to wipe away her tears.

Raj reassured her, "It is fine. We still have five more hours. Come on, let us keep on going."

But deep down in his heart, he was frightened too.

1:16 AM

Raj and Dhana slowly crept in the vast jungle. All of a sudden Raj felt like the ground below him let go. He was falling into a deep pit! Raj tried grabbing some of the mud to stop his fall, but it broke off and he continued falling. The wet mud felt gooey in his nervous, sweaty hands. He quickly dropped it.

"Aaaaaaaaaahhhhh! Help me!" He screamed.

Dhana was very worried. *Was she going to lose Raj, too*? The pit was very deep and Dhana didn't know what to do.

Then, she got an idea! She decided to grab a vine and let it in the hole. She took a long vine and dropped it in. Raj jumped to reach for it. It was too short! Dhana raced back, and found a longer one. Raj took hold of it and climbed back out. Raj was just laying down.

That was close, he thought. *What other things will I face tonight?*

They went deeper into the thick forest. Dhana was looking at a plant, while Raj was viewing the other side. All of a sudden, Dhana let out a scream. She was sprawled on the ground, like she tripped on something.

"Are you okay? What happened?" Raj questioned.

Dhana replied, "I tripped on some plant or rock. It really hurts."

She got up, but her knee was sprained. She just sat back down on the floor. She uprooted the plant and was going to fling it when she froze. Her eyes widened, and a few seconds later, she was up and dancing.

"Watch out for your knee! Get back down!" Raj scolded.

Dhana obeyed, and handed the plant over. "Our mission is complete!" she said with joy and happiness.

Raj gasped. It was a Kapikachu plant! And this time, for real. He felt like he was going to faint, but he held steady and walked towards Dhana. They were both happy for the first time this night.

"Let's go save Dad!" Raj said. And with that, they were off!

4:46 AM

The two kids retraced their steps back. A chill went down Raj's back. Even though it was almost bright, Raj felt nervous and frightened. His heart was beating as fast as a rabbit's. It was so quiet, he heard the crickets chirping. He cautiously tip-toed through the bushes of the tiger. He felt like it was going to pounce any moment. All of a sudden, they touched something other than the bushes… something moving. Dhana started screaming, but Raj put a hand over her mouth.

"Sssshhhhh. It might be the tiger." Raj whispered.

They slowly crept back, and Raj showed the lantern. Nothing was found. They bumped into something again. There was another scream.

"Dhana, I told you to be quiet."

"That wasn't me. I don't sound like that!"

It was true, this sounded like an older person. Raj turned around, and there facing him was a scared person. Raj immediately recognized this hurt human as his mom! Raj felt wobbly, his legs were shaking. He had to pinch himself to make sure it wasn't a dream. And—ow—it was reality.

"Mom?" the kids blurted out at the same time.

"Raj? Dhana?" she stared in shock. "I thought you were a tiger...or worse!"

Raj was so relieved! "You're alive!" he yelled, putting his arms around her neck.

Lakshmi hugged and kissed both of her kids. As usual, Dhana started crying, but this time with tears of joy.

"Yes, I am. At the first, I smelt smoke, so I came in here to warn you. Turns out, I was in the wrong direction. Now, how did you get here?" Before either of them could even answer that, Lakshmi realized something. "Where's Dad?" she asked.

"Oh no! We have to hurry, he got bit by a snake. Could you please use this to heal him?" Dhana asked, handing her the Kapikachu.

"Yes, it's possible. But we need to go...now!"

They all ran towards Ramu, hoping it's not too late.

5:54 AM

They all came to the unconscious body of Ramu. Lakshmi then broke the plant seed and spread it on his wound. The next few minutes were the most suspenseful. Ramu's body was still, even though Lakshmi spread the cure.

Raj shivered. He thought, *we might be too late. Its 6:05!*

Dhana sobbed, leaning over her dad, "Dad? Dad! Please! I need you!!"

Her wet tears landed on Ramu's wrinkled cheeks. Slowly, but surely, his face twitched to the wet drops.

"Dad!" Dhana cried with joy.

Ramu's eyes fluttered, then opened. Everything was blurry for him. He was hoping to see two faces staring back, but instead, there were three! He tried to believe it, but he couldn't.

"Lakshmi?" he groaned.

His whole body ached, but it was still worth it. They all helped him up. Raj and his mom held both of his hands for support, and Dhana held Lakshmi's. Together, they chatted and slowly stumbled into the jungle.

Now, the entire family was complete.

6:37 AM

Ramu was feeling a bit better now. Even though it still hurt, it was nothing compared to what the family faced. As usual, Raj and Dhana were squabbling over their adventures. Inside, both of them had pride, the pride they deserved. They both realized, "In twelve hours, so many things happened! A lost mom, a dad bitten by a snake, a tiring but adventurous journey through the forest, and a lot more. It was too much for a ten and seven-year-old to handle."

Raj once heard someone say, "Love will always find a way." And yes, it did. The four faint, but happy, figures disappeared in the crack of dawn, looking for yet another adventure.

Personification

Ellen Kazimer mentored Maryam Ali through a revision using personification to sculpt her poem, *I Love Spring*.

Dear Reader,

One of the things I love about poetry is that it makes us look at the world in new and ingenious ways. Often a poet employs figurative language (metaphor, simile, assonance, alliteration, or personification) to make us wonder anew. In her poem, *I Love Spring*, Maryam Ali uses personification to bring spring to life running, playing, and dancing.

Isn't this a marvelous approach to characterizing spring?

Our focus for revision was to bolster personification by adding a new stanza and strengthening the existing ones. To generate revision ideas, I asked Maryam to consider the five senses, touch, taste, smell, sound, and sight, as she revised her stanzas and created a new one. Her original poem used the sense of sight, but her final poem included smell, taste, and sound as well. Spring sings and makes strawberries taste yummy.

For fun, try personifying an element of nature, an inanimate object, or an animal. For example, how would you personify water, a window, or a wallaby? Would your water cry? Would your windows be watchful? Would your wallaby go on a walkabout?

Here are three other poems you may enjoy that employ personification.

Fog, by Carl Sandburg

Batty, by Shel Silverstein

The Giving Tree, by Shel Silverstein

Maryam did a commendable job blending her original vision with new ideas. It takes an open mind to re-envision your work. Then it takes considerable grit to rewrite any piece of writing you have already poured your heart into. Lastly, it takes understanding about yourself as a writer and about the work you are creating. Maryam had an open mind, grit, and understanding.

I hope you enjoy *I Love Spring* as much as I did and envision spring running, playing, and bringing the season to life.

Happy writing,

Ellen Kazimer

Ellen Kazimer self-published her first book back in first grade using construction paper, crayons and safety pins for binding. At the time, she could draw better than she could write. Since then, her writing has improved, but alas, her drawing skills have not. A Navy veteran and former teacher, she writes short stories, picture books, poetry, novels, and nonfiction. Occasionally she attempts to draw or paint something. She holds an MA in Writing for Children and Young Adults from Hamline University, and an MS in Operations Research from the Naval Postgraduate School.

Maryam Ali

Homeschooler Maryam Ali is in the third grade. Her favorite subjects are art and science. She loves learning about outer space, particularly the planets and stars. She enjoys visiting museums especially the Space Center in Houston. Maryam's favorite books are encyclopedias. In addition to writing, her hobbies are drawing, martial arts and tennis. She is also fond of solving puzzles, riddles, and doing word searches.

Ellen Kazimer: When did you start writing poetry?

Maryam Ali: Two years ago, when I started homeschooling. I think I was 7.

Q: How do you come up with your ideas?

A: I think of things that I like, and then I write about them.

Q: Who do you share your poetry with?

A: Mostly I share it with my Mom, and in my writing classes with my homeschooler friends. I have a journal I write and draw in.

Q: Are you working on any new poems?

A: I wrote two yesterday. One poem is about winter, which is another of my favorite seasons. The other is about a pony. I drew the pony first,

and then I wrote the poem. The pony's name is "Star Bright Shimmer," and that is the name of the poem.

Q: How did you feel about revising your poem for the contest?
A: It was hard because I thought my poem was perfect and then I had to change it.

Q: What advice do you have for other young poets?
A: It is easier to write when you have ideas already. Think about what you like and why. Write about those things. Then put the words together in a poem.

I Love Spring

by

Maryam Ali

The sun is shining up so high;
The grass is soft and green.
The flowers are blooming to catch sunlight.
Oh Spring! Spring is here!

Spring is running down the hill.
I follow her to see
How she makes the flower buds
Bloom so beautifully.

Spring is dancing behind the bush.
I dance with her to see
How she turns the strawberries red
And make them taste yummy!

Spring is playing with animals.
I try to play with them but see
How all the animals run to her.
Why don't they play with me?

Spring is singing in the trees.
I sing with her to see
How the birds chirp melodiously
The same rhythm and beat.

Spring is packing up her bags
And getting ready to leave.
I give her a rose to plant and keep red
So she will remember me!

Action-Reaction

Kristi Wright helped Natalie Wong examine her characters' reactions to things that happened her story, *Discovering Magic*, in order to show the complexity of her characters' lives.

Dear Reader,

In *Discovering Magic*, Natalie Wong's protagonist Audrey, must come to grips with a magical world she never dreamed possible. It was a delight to mentor Natalie, not only because her story hooked me immediately, but also because she was so open to the revision process.

For Natalie's revision, we focused on ACTION-REACTION (also known as STIMULUS-RESPONSE). The idea is that every action has a reaction (not unlike stimulus-response in science). Often we write wonderful actions and then forget to let our characters fully react to them. Unfortunately, our readers will notice when this happens and they may feel let down.

Basically, every action must have a character-appropriate reaction. Likewise, if there's a reaction in your story, then you must have already shown the action (or stimulus) that provoked it. If you don't think the reaction will make sense to the reader, then you should explain it via dialogue or by using the character's interior thoughts. Finally, if there's a reflexive reaction, like a shudder or a scream, it should probably happen first before any other reaction.

For example:

Action:

Sam barreled up to Alex, punched her in the shoulder, and said, "Hey!"

Possible reactions:

Best friends: *Alex smiled and said, "Hey" back.*

Sworn enemies: *"Ow!" said Alex. "Do that again and you lose an arm."*

Never seen each other in their life—in this case, we need to know what Sam is thinking: *Whoa! That's Alex, thought Sam. The jerk who broke her best friend's nose. She barreled up to Alex and punched her in the shoulder. Alex screeched. Then she punched Sam back.*

We analyzed Natalie's manuscript and discovered some great revision opportunities. For example, in the beginning, Audrey sees a car with a nautilus shell design on it. Then she goes home, opens a letter from her grandmother, and finds a stone with the same design! That's a coincidence you'd expect Audrey to notice.

Here's the original text:

Besides the feel of the stone, the most interesting thing by far was the beautiful nautilus shell. The detail was extensive, even though it looked to be barely one square inch wide and long.

And here's Natalie's revision:

Besides the feel of the stone, the most interesting thing

by far was the beautiful nautilus shell. The detail was extensive, even though it looked to be barely one square inch wide and long. Remembering the car with the nautilus shell on it, Audrey pondered whether or not the two were connected, but before she could fully explore her train of thought, a noise came from downstairs.

Now consider your own work. Highlight actions that happen in your manuscript. Are characters reacting to these actions? Are they reacting in a way that makes sense? Are complicated reactions explained via interior thoughts or dialogue?

To misquote Sir Isaac Newton, for every action, there is an appropriate reaction!

Happy Writing,

Kristi Wright

Kristi Wright is an Assistant Regional Advisor in the Society of Children's Books Writers and Illustrators. She offers writing workshops at the elementary school level with a focus on viewpoint and sensory detail. She is also the assistant editor for a blog that does craft analysis of children's literature: www.kidlitcraft.com. Her indie-published middle grade adventure series, *The Basker Twins in the 31st Century*, raises funds and awareness for a rare, childhood-onset disease, Friedreich's ataxia. She lives in Northern California with her husband and three furry friends. Find her at www.kristiwrightauthor.com and on Instagram/Twitter @KristiWrite.

Natalie Wong

Natalie Wong is thirteen years old and a seventh grader at Castilleja. She lives in Los Altos with her parents, twin, and younger sister. Natalie loves to read and eat dark chocolate. Currently, her favorite pop artist is BTS, although she also likes many instrumental sound tracks. She is a huge fan of the *Harry Potter* series, and was lucky enough to be able to see the original Broadway cast of *Harry Potter and the Cursed Child* perform in New York! Natalie also plays soccer, can play piano, and speak some Mandarin, a tiny bit of Spanish, and a few words of Korean.

Kristi Wright: What inspired you to write *Discovering Magic*?

Natalie Wong: My idea came from pretty much out of the blue! It was very spontaneous, but I think that because I like fantasy, it also contributed to my writing of the story.

Q: When you submitted your story to Young Inklings, you mentioned that you really liked planning out this story before you began to write. Can you speak more about that process? How did you go about planning your plot?

A: Well, when I was writing the story, I kind of started it then went along and wrote whatever came to mind. The planning element refers to how each occurrence, generally between the stone, Audrey, and the villain, had hints and clues about what was to come. For example, when Audrey is in City & State and the fly starts bothering her, this hinted that the villain was attempting to—oops! No spoilers!

Q: What was your favorite part of *Discovering Magic*?
A: I loved writing about Audrey's time at City & State when she's with her friends, because I based this pretty much entirely off personal experiences with my friends at a complex called Town & Country. Being able to put a little bit of my life into the story was pretty cool.

Q: How did you feel about focusing on Action-Reaction (Stimulus-Response) for your revision?
A: The focus on Action-Reaction (Stimulus-Response) was so incredibly helpful to me! As I was making revisions, I could tell that this concept would come in handy even later in life, not just in the moment. Action-Reaction is really important because it adds depth and grounds the story too, so that the fantasy elements aren't so crazy that it sounds completely fake and impossible.

Q: Did you learn anything from this revision process that you can use as you write your next story?
A: I learned how to apply the Action-Reaction concept, which will definitely be useful in the future.

Q: What advice would you give other writers about revision?
A: Dive right into it! Revision is NOT because your story is bad. It's because your story is SO GOOD that people want you to WRITE MORE ABOUT IT! That's the way I try to approach it.

Q: How long have you been writing?
A: I only really started liking writing since second grade. I lost a little bit of interest during fifth grade, then got back into it at sixth grade.

Q: What are some of your favorite books?
A: *Harry Potter*!!! I love all of the books in the series!

Q: What other things do you like to do besides write and read books?
A: I like to listen to BTS music (my family thinks I'm weird because I like their music!) as well as various instrumental tracks and eat good food, including sushi and chocolate. Reading while eating, when possible, is also fun.

Discovering Magic

by

Natalie Wong

Audrey Coven hurried happily along the cement sidewalk on the way home from school, a white envelope clutched in her hand. It was a letter from Granny, Audrey's beloved grandmother, who always managed to surprise her favorite (and only) granddaughter with sweet surprises. Audrey could picture her now, smiling a bright smile and busying herself somehow, with her trademark pearl necklace swinging around her neck.

Audrey investigated the envelope, and she could feel a little trinket that seemed strangely smooth. Then a sleek black car caught her eye that was pulling into the driveway of the house three doors down from hers. Its engine grumbled, then sighed and was abruptly cut off. The most curious thing about the car was that it had a nautilus shell carved onto the side of it.

Huh, Audrey thought. It wasn't every day that you saw cars with nautilus shells on them.

A woman in a black skirt, leggings, a shirt, and a neat jacket that

perfectly matched the car she'd seemed to come out of appeared on the far side of the car. The funny thing about her attire was the strange silver pin that she wore, shining brightly against her otherwise dull clothing. Audrey was too far away to make out any words or symbols on the pin. The woman briskly knocked on the door of the house that owned the driveway and appeared to be welcomed into the home.

Taking no more interest, Audrey sprinted past the last few houses to her house for fun and let herself inside. Her parents were both out at work, and she had no siblings or pets, so for the time being, Audrey had the entire Coven house to herself.

Running upstairs to her bedroom, she dropped her book-laden backpack beside her desk, tore open the letter, and let the contents fall to the floor.

What fell out was a strange, smooth black stone and a scrap of paper with her Granny's familiar, curved handwriting on it. The stone had a shell pictured on it, while Granny's note only contained a few words: *For the best. Lots of love, Granny.*

Disappointed and thoroughly confused, Audrey sat down, ignoring her backpack, which had fallen over from the sheer amount of weight it contained.

First, she turned the note over and over, trying to find a hidden meaning or more words, but could find nothing except the vague message that she'd seen at first.

On to the stone. Audrey felt the texture beneath her fingers; smooth and strangely…sparky?… At the same time. *Sparky* was the only worked that described the reaction her skin had when it touched the stone, like static electricity, but somehow different. It wasn't painful, but Audrey decided to be more cautious when handling the stone in the future.

Besides the feel of the stone, the most interesting thing by far was the beautiful nautilus shell. The detail was extensive, even though it looked to be barely one square inch wide and long. Remembering the car with the nautilus shell on it, Audrey pondered whether or not the two were connected, but before she could fully explore her train of thought, a noise came from downstairs.

Audrey heard a door creak open and push shut.

"HELLO?" Audrey's mother called. The sound of footsteps from the ruby-red Nike shoes her dad always wore came soon after, though he didn't yell a greeting like her mom.

"COMING!" Audrey yelled back. Now she would have to help heat up dinner. Audrey hurriedly stuffed the stone and note into her school backpack.

She dragged herself downstairs.

"Hey, honey," her dad said. "How was school?"

"Good," Audrey mumbled in reply.

"You're not allowed to use that word anymore," her mom reminded her. "Give us a better description."

Audrey sighed inwardly. *What more could be expressed without using the simple word 'good'?*

"Oh yeah!" she exclaimed. She had remembered the black car. *Finally, a newsworthy topic!*

"I saw a cool black car today. It even had this nautilus shell on the sides, and a woman in black clothes with a funny silver pin on her jacket came out of it," she explained.

Normally, her parents would react by asking her more questions and coming up with crazy hypothetical scenarios involving

the topic. But this time, they both froze for a moment, with looks of anxiety on their faces. Her mom's eyebrows creased and her lips were tight, and she nervously rubbed her panda-shaped wedding ring, while her dad agonizingly ran his hand through his hair and tapped his shoes with a distinctly worried movement.

Audrey was surprised. She didn't expect her parents to react in this way. They recovered quickly, though, and tried to regain their former composure.

"Cool, huh? Is the food cold?" her mom asked.

Audrey frowned slightly. The leftover pasta that was for dinner had been heated up only a few seconds ago, and was still steaming on the table.

Something was up. And Audrey was determined to figure it out.

When Audrey woke the next morning, the light shone unusually bright through the curtains blocking the window across from her bed. Groggy with leftover remnants of sleep, she sleepily checked her watch. The blinking digital screen read 6:50 am, Friday. Suddenly sitting up, Audrey muttered about how stupid she was to have slept through her alarm. It must not have been loud enough, because she was sure she'd set one on her watch the night before. She had to get to school by 7:15 am, so it was time to rush!

Pushing away all thoughts of alarms, Audrey concentrated on rushing through her normally more relaxed wake-up routine: get up, get dressed, brush teeth, eat breakfast, get school stuff, walk to school. Because she had accidentally slept in, the schedule was reduced to: get up, throw clothes on, swirl mouthwash, eat a banana, grab backpack, and sprint to school.

When Audrey finally arrived at her locker (number 77), clutching a cramp in her side, it was 7:18 am. She quickly threw all her school books into her locker and checked her planner for the first class period, which turned out to be Spanish. Audrey groaned. The classroom was on the third floor of a building halfway across campus. She could make it, but only just.

Running full-out with all of her Spanish items, Audrey hurtled into the classroom at exactly 7:20, right on time with the rest of the class and her friend, Del. Del's real name was Delilah, but Audrey and the rest of her friends (Jamie, CeeCee, and Jill) called her Del for short.

"Where've you been?" Del whispered as the teacher, Ms. Hudson, began the class by reviewing the conjugations for past tense verbs.

"Woke up late," Audrey gasped, pulling out her homework.

As Ms. Hudson walked by collecting homework, she took Audrey's paper and gave her an approving smile.

It wasn't until the recess break after Spanish and History that Audrey got to mentally regroup at her locker. Digging around in her backpack, she felt Granny's note, which she had stuffed in the night before. Strangely, she didn't feel the stone.

All of a sudden, a funny feeling overtook her. She felt as though her mind was reaching out, searching for the stone, while the stone was simultaneously calling her name.

Audrey. Audrey. Audrey, it whispered.

Whipping her head around to the left, Audrey just had time to see some students disappear around a corner and the stone drop onto the floor at the end of the hall.

What is happening to me? Audrey thought. Ever since the stone had arrived, life just kept getting weirder and weirder.

For a moment, it seemed as though Audrey and the stone were the only beings left in the eerily quiet hallway while other students moved silently and in slow motion around them. Then the hallway suddenly lurched and twisted, and things were back to normal again.

What just happened? Audrey asked herself.

Just then, the school bell rang, shocking Audrey out of her stupor of confusion about what had just taken place.

She inconspicuously snatched the stone up, stuffed it in her jacket pocket, then made her way to her next class.

"Hey guys, does anybody want to come to City & State with me after school?" Del asked.

City & State was the nearby shopping and eating center.

Jamie, CeeCee, and Jill immediately responded with a synchronized and enthusiastic "yes", but Audrey took out her phone (an iPhone 6. It was pretty much an artifact.) and texted her parents.

"Sorry, just a second guys," she apologized to her friends.

"No problemo, mi amiga! It's all good," Jill replied.

A reply came a second later. It said, "Yes, you can go, but get back to the house by 4:15!"

A curfew? Audrey had never had one before.

She texted back, "Why?" but, after receiving no reply for a

minute with her friends awkwardly waiting for her, she gave up and announced that she could go.

With a cup of chocolate ice cream and some garlic fries in hand, Audrey and her friends sat down at a bench surrounded by colorful flower pots to eat the snacks they'd bought. The instant the garlic fries were set down on the table, Jamie snatched one out. CeeCee and Audrey both pretended to attack Jamie, while Jill took advantage of their distraction and snagged two fries. It was all in good fun, and Audrey felt content to sit there and eat unhealthy, sugar-filled foods with her friends forever.

However, she slowly became aware of something that seemed to be poking her on her side. Lifting her arm and looking, she saw that a poor little fly seemed to be drawn into her pocket. Audrey deftly swatted it away, and the fly buzzed off to do other things.

Jill, CeeCee, Audrey, and Jamie sat discussing school for a while, as well as Jill's upcoming volleyball tournament. All too soon, Audrey checked her watch and realized that it was 4:00. She would have to leave now in order to get back to her house at 4:15.

"Sorry guys, but I gotta go now," she said.

"Okay! Bye Audrey! See you on Monday!" her friends chorused.

Audrey slung her backpack on, trashed the ice cream cup, and started walking briskly in the direction of her home. As she rounded a corner to exit City & State, a grown woman dressed all in black suddenly bumped into her.

"Oh! Sorry!" Audrey quickly said.

The woman didn't even reply, and Audrey watched as she

simply strode past Audrey, clutching something tightly in her hand. The item she was holding suddenly caught a ray of sunlight, and a nautilus shell carved onto a smooth black surface flashed into Audrey's eyes.

Audrey, it said.

Then time seemed to slow down again. The woman had stolen the stone!

Audrey didn't know if she wanted to scream for help or run. This was all too weird for her. Time doesn't slow down. Stones don't whisper to you. People don't try to steal whispering stones from you!

But it was all happening again, right before Audrey's very confused eyes. She felt as though she had to do something to get the stone...but what?

You know, said the stone's eerie, yet comforting voice.

And Audrey did. She extended her arm, fingers stretched towards the stone, and imagined the stone coming to her open hand. It obeyed instantly, and shot into her hand. As soon as skin and stone touched, Audrey closed her hand around the black stone and casually plopped it right back into her pocket –but left her hand in the pocket so that no one could take it again.

And then she recognized the woman who had tried to take the stone. She was the same one that had come out of the black car the day before.

Feeling like more mysteries than ever were popping up around her, Audrey spent the rest of the walk home thinking about the stone as well as the strange encounters she'd had that day.

One: Why did the woman want the stone?

Two: What did the nautilus shell mean?

Three: Why did Granny send it to Audrey?

Four: What did the note mean?

Five: Was it dangerous for Audrey to keep the stone? Should she get rid of it?

As soon as the last, treacherous question entered her mind, Audrey pushed it away. Even if strange, even dangerous, things happened around the stone, she felt a sort of attachment to it now, as though if she gave it up she would never forgive herself for it, and the stone wouldn't either.

Finally: Should she tell her parents?

They had reacted strangely when Audrey told them about the car, so she was hesitant to tell them that more unexplained phenomenons had been occurring. She decided that it was best to keep her encounters with the stone a secret.

It was just before Audrey's bed time, and she had already turned out the light and started getting into bed when her window creaked. Audrey froze for a second, but dismissed it and continued to wrap herself up in her sheets, as it was a cold night, even though the heat was on.

Then the window shifted. The glass panes actually moved to Audrey's left and the stinging night air rushed in.

Then the stone started whispering again. *Audrey.*

A lithe black animal was squeezing its way through the small gap the window had left when it moved. It was sickening, watching it coil and twist, her body unable to move for fear, until it dropped to the floor with a muffled thump. Audrey wanted to scream, but couldn't.

It was a snake. A night-black king cobra, to be exact. The nauseating sound of hissing filled the room, and Audrey finally managed to yell, "AHHHH!!!!"

It wasn't very dignified, but what else could you do when confronted with window-moving snakes?

The stone kept whispering. *Audrey. Audrey. Audrey.*

Audrey finally rushed to her backpack and took the stone out, clutching it protectively. The cobra, which had started to slide towards the backpack, reared up and started to... change. It thrashed as though it was in pain and the hissing grew louder as it elongated, curled in on itself, then burst out and grew. Legs, arms, and finally, a face appeared.

Audrey, the stone said.

The woman from the black car was standing in Audrey's room.

Gasping, Audrey stuttered and backed up to the door of her room. She felt for the handle as the woman smiled, showing blackened teeth, and stepped towards her.

"Don't go, dear. Really, it's all right," she crooned.

Audrey's hand was on the door handle, and she turned, but all of a sudden the woman lashed out with inhuman speed and wrenched her wrist away from the door, leaving a red mark on Audrey's hand. It wasn't bleeding, but it felt like poison, as though something horrible was slowly seeping into her. Shocked, Audrey rubbed the injured hand, trying in vain to push out the poison. She was sure that the substance would affect her badly somehow, but wasn't able to figure out exactly how.

The stone quivered and made a movement towards her injured wrist.

Let me heal you, it offered.

Understanding, Audrey moved the stone and pressed the shell, face down, onto the wrist. Within a few seconds, the mark was gone.

The woman had watched all this with the look of a scientist watching a lab rat on her face.

She pouted when the red mark melted away, and said, "Oh, I so hoped you wouldn't do that. It doesn't matter now, though. But let me start over. I am Mora. You may have…encountered me before crawling towards your jacket pocket or perhaps accidentally bumping into you—so sorry about that, by the way."

However kind Mora's words were, Audrey still got the distinct impression that Mora was completely unapologetic.

"If you would kindly hand over that worthless stone you're clutching, we can all forget this and be on our respective ways. Yes?" Mora finished.

Audrey.

Mora reached out a hand.

Audrey!

Audrey couldn't let Mora take the stone. She knew that the stone didn't want to go. So, she drunk up the dregs of her bravery and answered defiantly, "If the stone wasn't important, why would you want it?"

She could see annoyance flash in Mora's face. "Stop asking questions. Give. Me. The. Stone."

Audrey waited a moment and thought. Then she pretended to be scared.

"You…you won't hurt it, will you? The stone, I mean? And you

won't hurt me if I give it to you?" she squeaked, making her voice as quavery as possible.

Mora seemed satisfied with her show. "Yes, yes. Now just hand it over…" Mora purred convincingly.

Audrey slowly extended out her arm, but just before Mora could take it, Audrey had an instinct and she whipped her hand back behind her head then brought it forward with as much force as she could and slammed the stone, shell face up, into the carpet.

Instead of bouncing harmlessly then rolling to a stop as any normal rock would, the stone, glowing, cracked and burst. A magnificent, golden dragon burst from the remains and roared so loud that Audrey's ears would ring for a day after. Then the dragon turned its luminous, starry blue eyes on Audrey.

Thank you, it rumbled. Then it whipped its wings out as far as they could go and lunged towards Mora.

The evil woman shrieked and started to change again, this time into a fly. The dragon continued to hurtle towards the fast-moving fly Mora had become. Audrey clutched the wall even more tightly. She realized that the black fly looked creepily similar to the one that she'd swatted away at City & State.

"NO!" Audrey yelled. She tried to block the gap, but she was too far away.

Then the golden dragon was there, snatching the fly up in its mouth.

Then her parents were there, standing like they were up for a fight, a red ibis bird hovering next to her dad and a growling panda hunched next to her mom.

The dragon turned and spat out the sorry, spit-drenched fly–no, Mora–into a jar that had suddenly appeared out of nowhere.

The fly flew sulkily around the jar, banging into the walls in futile attempts to break free.

And the world was quiet again.

The entire animal and Coven family entourage was situated around the living room. Audrey's parents both took deep breaths, but before any one of them could open their mouths, both of them started sobbing and crying. Audrey sat stiffly, unsure of what to do. She was still in partial sensory overload.

Finally, the sobbing let up, and Audrey's mom began.

"Our last name, the word coven, means a group of witches, or people with certain… abilities." Audrey's mom stopped and took a deep breath, as though the next thing she was about to say held great weight.

"We both come from families that have the power to bond with objects. These objects contain things called manifests. There are different types of manifests, or you could think of them as animal companions. Each manifest has a specialty. Some of them are good with shape shifting, some with elemental wielding, and so on."

"That's right. Gully–" Audrey's dad pointed to the ibis. "Is my manifest. He takes the form of the red shoes I always wear. Your mom's manifest, Ling–"

The panda shifted when it heard its name.

"Ling takes the form of Mom's wedding ring. In terms of number, the population of manifests fluctuates according to non-manifests of the same species. And yes, that does mean non-manifest dragons exist in the real world."

Audrey's hand had shot into the air.

" I'm sorry Audrey, but put your hand down, and please just listen for now. All manifests start out as inanimate objects, and each type of manifest has one certain object it starts out as. Gully was a feather when he came to me! When a manifest is initiated, then you and the manifest may truly bond and choose a more permanent form."

Right then, Audrey's manifest, the dragon, seemed to puff up its chest. It gently nudged her dad, as though it wanted to tell Audrey something important.

Hello, Audrey. My name is Nova. I am your manifest, it—no, Nova—told her.

With this thought, Audrey felt a little twist of excitement making its way through her veins.

"Manifests usually arrive during someone's teenage years. And it just so happens, Audrey, that your manifest here…is a Golden Dragon."

"So, when Nova came to me, she was a nautilus shell carved on a stone." Audrey said. "Then I cracked the stone and initiated her. But why did Mora, who is the fly, want her?"

"There are some witches and wizards in the world who don't want to share their power with another being, as the manifest -human relationship is equally balanced. One half of the pair would be nowhere as powerful compared to their strength together. People who do not appreciate this relationship end up getting rid of their manifest. They steal others in their forms before they are initiated so they can take the power manifests hold. Mora, who you have told us is the fly, must have realized that Nova, who I assume to be your dragon manifest, was to come to you, and tried to steal Nova before you could initiate her," her mom replied.

Her parents both took a deep, synchronized breath, bringing the conversation to a halt.

Then Audrey, who had been emotionally dormant throughout the whole talk, suddenly burst into tears. It was all so weird, crazy, and unreal, but yet it was true. All of it was real, and even though it was incredibly scary, it was also…surprising. Exciting. A whole new world full of opportunities! Already she felt a special connection to Nova.

Her parents huddled around her, comforting her with their embraces.

"It's okay. We'll figure it out," they murmured. "It's okay."

And just for that moment, Audrey was content to believe them.

Back in her bed, with Nova in the form of a gold-plated dragon necklace, Audrey decided that it was time to try to make her own sense of the world her parents had revealed to her—and she still had so many unanswered questions!

However, the energy she had used from the day was spent, and she could feel her eyes closing, too heavy with exhaustion to stay open.

As Audrey drifted into the hazy realm of sleep, she promised herself that she would never become like Mora. No matter what, she and Nova would stick together, and they could take on any evil witch or wizard the world sent their way.

THE END

Character Motivation

Megan White guided Kaia Lucas on revising to better reveal her characters' motivations in her story, *The Storm Ship*.

Dear Reader,

The most important part of any story is the characters. Without interesting people for your readers to care about, even the most amazing plots and settings won't make a story perfect. For Kaia's story, with an amazing setting and a crazy-fun plot, we decided to focus on what motivated her characters, so we could make all of their adventures and decisions make sense and seem important to the reader.

Adeline's mother in this story is a cruel, mean woman who abuses Adeline and forces her to run away from home. But why was she so violent and scary? We brainstormed ideas to build up important scenes that could provide a history for these characters. This way, readers can understand the reasons why characters act the way they do.

History for characters can either be clearly explained in a story, written in with detail, or it can be implied, meaning you can drop in little hints about things that happened so your reader has to fill in the blanks for themselves. It's up to the writer to decide which parts are important enough to include fully and which parts to make the reader work a little harder for!

We also talked about the importance of keeping things a little bit simpler. In early drafts of Kaia's story, there were some additional characters that weren't necessarily helpful towards the main focus of the story. These extra characters made the motivation for the main characters a little bit confusing, so in the end, they were taken out. Getting rid of some of these extra pieces can be hard, especially if you like them, but the effect on your story is that your readers get to focus completely on what's important.

You can also use vocabulary to emphasize certain things about characterization. Try going through your story, and see what kind of words you use to describe each character and their actions. For a villain, you want to use words that show how evil they really are, and for a hero, you want to emphasize how good they are. See if you can use different words for these different characters, and your readers will feel much more strongly about them and see the differences between them much more clearly without even picking up on why right away!

Your characters are the backbone of your story, so try some of these things to make them stand out as individuals and be more memorable to your readers!

Happy writing!

Megan White

Megan White is a college student at Skidmore, in New York. She grew up writing, and is currently majoring in creative writing and hopes to work in publishing someday. She has been a part of the Society of Young Inklings since she was seven years old! Her hobbies include hiking, reading, writing, and getting lost in the depths of Netflix.

Kaia Lucas

Kaia is an awkward, weird girl at the beginning of her metamorphosis. She spends her days reading, video gaming, and daydreaming of the future in which she has a younger sister. At school, she is endlessly tormented by teachers who give deadlines (darn teachers and their love for overworking students!). She spends most of her time at school daydreaming, instead of doing actual work. She's excited to have a story published for the first time.

Megan White: How much did you change when you were revising your story?

Kaia Lucas: I'd say quite a bit. A lot of the changes were small words that I was like, "Do I really need those words?" So a lot of the work was just changing tiny little things. I took some pieces out and added others in, but some of my changes were really big sentences and other important elements of the story. I'd say I did quite a bit of revising!

Q: Did if surprise you how much you wanted to change?

A: It did surprise me, because often when I first look at a story, I think it is just fine and doesn't need revision. But then when I get a chance to look at it further, I realize that it does need revising. I'm glad I looked closer at this story.

Q: What was your process for changing things?

A: For me, I tried to get a system with colors and stuff, but I'm not really the kind of person who works well with a whole process. So, I just kind of saw stuff that I wanted to change and made the edits and revisions.

Q: What is your favorite part of revising? Your least favorite?

A: My least favorite is admitting to myself that parts that I really like don't need to be in there. My favorite is probably looking at a part that I changed. At the end of my revising for a day, I can look back and be really proud of myself, because I did really good revising that day and everything I changed was for a good reason.

Q: How do you come up with your ideas?

A: When I wrote this story, I was so interested in ships and female pirates and female heroines and family relationships, and I still am interested in a lot of that stuff. I just found it really easy to get the story flowing. It was pretty easy to find ideas, because I could just look around and catch tidbits of stories and see what the people look like and what they were doing. I could see words and come up with ideas!

Q: Do you have any advice for other people trying to write and revise stories?

A: Don't try to compare yourself to others. It's never a good idea! It's always going to make you think your work is not as good, or a copy of someone else's. Then, you just feel worse about your work and not good about it like you should.

The Storm Ship

by

Kaia Lucas

Adeline De Rouge looked up to the emerald skies of Terre de Couleur. She crooned a lullaby that her younger sister had taught her. "Douce lune, dans le ciel, regarde au-dessus de moi…" Green light filtered in through the window. In Terre de Couleur, the skies were always different colored, yellow one day, purple the other.

Adeline brushed back a strand of her jet-black hair and looped one of her long, elegant arms around her sister Lydia, who was fast asleep. Lydia, who looked nothing like her sister, had fair skin, periwinkle eyes, and short blonde hair. However, Lydia was slim and graceful like Adeline, with long, slender fingers, perfect for piano playing. Adeline, however, had tan skin with envy-green eyes and jet-black hair like a murder of crows.

The day was silent and perfect. It was almost night, however, and Adeline knew she had skipped piano practice. She didn't care, because she hated piano practice. Still, she gripped the handle of her teacup harder. Adeline knew this peace wouldn't last forever, so she

would have to cherish it while it did.

"Sigh…if I were to invent…say…an IRON SHIP, would my family care?" She asked herself. But she knew the answer. They wouldn't. She was a mistake. To prove her point, her mother barged in.

"ADELINE!" She screamed. "YOU AGAIN HAVE SKIPPED PIANO PRACTICE!"

Adeline pouted. Her mother's name was Reese De Rouge. She had mousy brown hair and tiny piggy eyes set on a face with a permanent sneer. She half pitied her mother. The hardships she had been through were the stuff of nightmares.

"But, mother…"

"NO BUTS!" Her mother took out a sharp metal knife, its blade gleaming in the light of the moon.

Adeline felt the scar over her face, tracing the shaky line. A memory, the first memory, came to her.

"No, Mother. HELP!" She was distracted when her mother reached for her, brandishing the knife.

Adeline dove to the side as her mother threw the knife, just barely missing her leg.

"STOP, MOTHER!" she bellowed.

Her mother stopped in a disorganized haze. Adeline could practically see memories coming, just for a moment, into her mother's head.

"Please," Adeline said. "Please, Mother."

"The time for please ended eleven years ago." Her mother choked. "He wanted Lydia not you. You were terrible, so he ran away."

"That's not true!" Adeline cried.

"It is and you know it." Her mother wheezed, exhausted from

chasing Adeline around the room. "Lydia…wasn't…old enough to…make him want to…leave…"

Adeline raced to her room, where she collapsed into her bed. She reached for the apple tree she had grown in secret, for when she would skip supper, and picked a gleaming, red apple. Suddenly, there was a knock on the door. Adeline hid the apple under her bed.

"Come in," she said. It was Lydia.

"I just came to bring you supper."

"Oh," Adeline sighed. "You didn't have to."

"I know, but you need food. You're going to starve," Lydia said, with a hint of worry in her voice. "It's vegetable soup. Please eat up."

Adeline carefully took the spoon and platter from her sister. She saw her reflection in the mirror, her jet-black hair, the scar over one of her bright green eyes.

"Thank you, Lydia," she said, her voice barely more than a whisper.

"You're welcome," Lydia said. Instead of closing the door to leave, she sat next to Adeline. "Let me guess. Mother tried to beat you up again," Lydia acknowledged, her voice gentle and kind.

"Of course!" Adeline snapped. "She hates me for existing!"

Lydia flinched. "Adeline…I'm so sorry."

"You don't have to be," Adeline grumbled, "I'm going to run away."

Lydia gasped. "NO! Adeline, you can't."

Adeline took a spoonful of soup. "I have to. I will sneak out and steal a ship tonight. You can come with me if you want."

Lydia sighed, "Okay."

"Okay?" Adeline asked.

"Yes."

"But weren't you just telling me off for doing it?"

"Yes," Lydia said. "But if you are going, I will go too. If I don't go, you will come back, and mother will kill you, literally."

Adeline felt an inexplicable, strong surge of anger at this. Lydia was so…perfect. She was so…not.

"Well, I'm going to go," Adeline whispered. "Come on."

"All right, I'll go pack some things," Lydia said.

"Go quickly!" Adeline cried out. *Lydia takes hours to pack!*

She opened the window and dropped to the ground. Terre de Couleur was stunning at night. Little shops and homes were crowded onto La Grâce Street, their lights slowly fading, shops closing and families going to bed. In the clear night sky, the moon and stars shone brightly, illuminating the streets. The docks were only a mile away. She could get a ship out to sea before 12:30 am.

"Adeline!" called Lydia, hauling three trunks behind her. "Wait up! One of these is for you!" She handed a shabby-looking trunk to Adeline, panting heavily all the way.

"Which way did you get out?" Adeline asked suspiciously.

"The front door, of course."

"Lydia! The front door makes too much noise! Mother will notice sooner!" Adeline scolded.

"Sorry," said Lydia sheepishly. Sure enough, Adeline heard the sounds of her mother awakening. If her father hadn't been missing since Lydia was two days old he would have saved her. Luckily her mother tripped on the stairs while coming down.

However, once she had gotten up, she looked out the door. Adeline and Lydia ducked out of sight, but her mother seemed to have seen them.

"Adeline!" Her mother boomed. "GIVE BACK YOUR SISTER, NOW!"

Adeline dashed to the docks. She scanned the docks for a ship. Rowboat? No. Sail boat? No. No, no, no…

"A-ha!" she cried and ducked into a ship called The Kraken. She let loose the sails and drifted away.

Adeline watched as the city shrunk into tiny dots before her, then finally disappeared. She turned to Lydia. "Do you actually think this is a good idea?" she asked.

Lydia shrugged. "I will miss mother, but I won't miss the scary… feeling."

"What feeling?" Adeline asked.

"I saw every time mother attacked you. I had to watch her break. Every time she lunged for you, I thought the next time was sure to be me." Lydia shivered.

Adeline snorted. "You didn't even think about me? About what it was like to have our own mother lunge at us with a look of total hatred, of complete unloving on her face?"

"I did!" Lydia frowned at her with such an innocent, frustrated and partially bewildered look on her face that Adeline had to admit she looked like she meant it. "But…it was scary. It was hard to do anything except hide it out, so I did."

"All right," Adeline whispered. "I'm going to look below deck for supplies," she whispered to Lydia, creeping down the stairs. She jumped as the bottom step let out a crreeaakk. She heard the snores of the crew, deep in sleep.

Wait. A crew? Adeline thought. She tiptoed down the stairs to

find six sailors, all fast asleep in hammocks.

BANG! Startled, Adeline fell into the closest sailor. Startled again, she bumped into another, hence a game of human dominos.

"W-who are you?" Adeline stammered.

"And why should I reveal that information?" The lead sailor asked, frowning.

Adeline frowned right back.

"Fine. I'm Adriana Blaze. This is Constantine Blaze, Eloise Felipe, William Valerie, George Charles, and Leia Titus. Who are you?" the leader asked.

"I–I… I am Adeline London De Rouge, daughter of Robert De Rouge and Reese De Rouge, sister of Lydia Darius De Rouge," she said, the stammer in her voice now barely a tremble.

"Hello, Adeline," Adriana said. "Why, now, are you here?"

Adeline took a deep breath.

BANG!!! A rifle shot burst out of midair, nearly clipping Adeline's shoulder. She looked back to see a ship rapidly catching up to them. Cannons were blasting straight at them, and gunmen were posted on the deck. In the middle of this, their mother was standing, directing orders like a full war general.

How did my mother get her hands on a warship?! Adeline wondered. *No time for that*, she thought.

Adeline tried to remember all that she had read about boats and ships. "Okay! Constantine, grab the sheets! Adriana, man the wheel! Eloise, abaft the beam! William, to the cannons! George, to the crow's nest! Leia, starboard!"

Adriana scowled. "You don't happen to be the captain of this ship, do you?" she asked.

"No, but this is important!" Adeline cried, dashing about.

"No. I know how to work a ship." Adriana growled, but she stormed over to the wheel anyway.

BANG! BANG! BANG! She heard a scream from Constantine as a bullet lodged in his right arm, blood oozing from the hole with pus barely showing through. Adriana grabbed a bandage and wrapped it around his right arm. Panting heavily from trying to steer the ship, sweat dripping down her face, and getting into her dark straight hair.

"Adeline! Help Constantine. All he needs is a well-put-on bandage and some bed rest, please."

Adeline heard the desperation in her voice. *They must be siblings*, she thought. She suddenly felt a pang of sadness for leaving her mother and her life behind. She could have found her father, so her mother would have gotten her sanity back. *But mother is too far off the deep end*. She reminded herself. *We wouldn't be able to really get her back*. She set Constantine down on a hammock.

"Don't worry, you're going to be…"

BOOM!!

That wasn't cannon fire, Adeline thought. "Stay right there, Constantine."

She ran out of the cabin and to the window. A storm was raging outside, the rain and thunder taunting the waves into a storm.

"Adriana!" she yelled. "Get Lydia and the rest of the crew into the cabin!"

"Yes, ma'am." Adriana mocked. "Wait. What's that?"

Sure enough, a ship was coming close. When it got close enough, Adeline could see the telltale signs of a pirate ship. Adriana's face paled.

"W-what?! Pirates…?" she whispered. Suddenly, a gust of wind rocked the ship, sending it closer to the pirate ship. Lydia screamed as the pirates lowered a drawbridge. Adeline rushed to the side of the ship to defend it.

"All hands hoay!" yelled the captain of the pirate ship.

From afar Adeline could see just a blurred figure, but when he got closer she could see that he had gnarled white-blonde hair that was twisted into dreadlocks. His eyes were an ice blue that Adeline had never seen before, reflecting the blue-black water and making them appear darker.

He twisted his mouth, which had zigzag scars running across it, into a snarl. "Kill them all."

He pointed at their ship, which revealed that instead of a hand, he had a scarred, tender stump that had probably once been covered by a hook, but that hook had been recently taken off for some reason. He was wearing two silver earrings in one ear, and three large hooped gold ones in the other.

He pointed again at Adeline's ship, this time more specifically her.

"Go," he snarled again, making the pirates rush on deck.

The crew of *The Kraken* unsheathed knives and put up their fists if they were not armed. Adriana, in addition to using a pocket knife, was smacking the pirates, leaving stinging red marks. Constantine had gotten out of bed to knee the pirates. George was dropping stones from the crow's nest. William and Eloise were head butting the pirates, and Leia was tripping them. Lydia helped George throw rocks, and Adeline smashed plates over their heads.

Thunder rumbled overhead, and lightning began to come

down from the sky, getting closer and closer to their boat. Adeline screamed as lightning hit the bridge between the two ships. The force of the blow sent *The Kraken* flying, blowing it totally off-course.

Adeline had flashbacks of screaming. Her screaming. Her mother sobbing.

Voices saying, "Adeline, come on…come on…"

Lydia screaming, "HELP!!!!" and most of all, the strange emptiness of her home.

She was crying out to parents that were gone. One literally, one's soul was just empty. She was falling into darkness…falling… falling…

Adeline woke up to the bright sun. Mild ship-wreckages were floating around, one of them from *The Kraken*. Her hand was wrapped in bandages, and she was lying in a cot on a sandy dune. She could see Lydia and the crew around her, some of them being attended to by people.

"Who…"

A young girl ran over to her. "Ah, you're awake," she said. "You'd best get out of bed, there are other people in your crew who need it more."

Adeline hoisted herself out of bed. She blinked and yawned. It was then that she saw the island. "Wow, it's beautiful!" she murmured.

The island was covered in forest, broken occasionally by a few wooden houses.

"I know," the girl said.

Adeline remembered the life she had left behind. There would be no more beatings, no more cruel taunts, but…she still loved her mother. She thought of her father, lost and probably looking for her.

This would mean abandoning all her family that she had left for good. At least on the ship, she had the option to turn back, to decide to stay with her mother. Even if it meant disappointing Lydia and her crew.

She hesitated, expecting to be turned down. "Can I…"

The girl looked at her quizzically, then seemed to figure out what she was asking for.

"Ah," she smiled. "Adeline, you can live here."

White Space

Tasslyn Magnusson mentored Caitlyn Zhu in using a poetic technique, white space, while revising her poem, *My Life in a Paper Bag*.

Dear Reader,

Poems are kind of extra special. We use words and images and phrases to evoke a scene, emotion, or idea. But we can also use the space on the page! Poets call it "white space." White space is all the space on the page that is NOT the poem. So how do you write a poem and use what looks like empty space on the page to write your poem?

I picked this revision focus because Caitlyn was already using the white space of her poem. She staggered words across the page and understood how white space could make the reader know important and not important words in her poem.

But to use the white space deliberately, we talked about some exercises Caitlyn should do. First, I asked her to move the stanzas left and right. Then, to read the stanzas out loud. Did that change her poem? Did it make her read faster or slower?

Next, Caitlyn and I looked at something called concrete

poems. Concrete poems are poems that are in the shape of their subject. Caitlyn had a stanza about a paintbrush. I asked her to try to put the paintbrush stanza in the shape of a paintbrush. Or the pencil, in the shape of the pencil. Concrete poems use white space on the page to enhance their subject.

We also walked about word choice. Which is weird, right? Because I said we were talking about the NOT poem part of the page. But when we think about poetry, we want to make sure each word is the exact right word and in the exact right space. Caitlyn wrote a beautiful line about a tiny stuffed penguin. "Tiny black eyes and a blue and white body peek out of my bag." She used alliteration and short words that helped me see this was a small animal. She used the spaces between words and the sounds and shapes of words to shape her poem.

The last thing I asked Caitlyn to do was think about line breaks. How and where you break lines in a poem can change the meaning of the poem. I asked Caitlyn to break up her lines and stanzas in different ways and experiment with adding mystery and suspense to her poem.

Caitlyn tried every single suggestion with her poem! I told her my rule—I try everything but I save my first draft and know I can always go back to it. I'm free to revise and experiment. Caitlyn did all of it—and we spent our second session reading her favorite versions she came up with. And she showed me some interesting experiments with concrete poetry she tried—which didn't work. But that's wonderful! Experimenting and playing and having fun are some of my favorite parts of being a poet.

Caitlyn—congratulations on a beautiful poem and extra congratulations on being a fearless reviser and experimenter!

Happy Revising to all!

Tasslyn Magnusson

Tasslyn Magnusson received her MFA in Creative Writing for Children and Young Adults at Hamline University in Saint Paul, MN. Her poems have been published or are forthcoming in *Broad River Review*, *Room Magazine*, *The Mom Egg Review*, *The Raw Art Review: A Journal of Storm and Urge*, and *Red Weather Online*. Her chapbook, *defining*, from dancing girl press was published in January 2019. She lives in Prescott, WI with her husband and two kids and two dogs.

Caitlyn Zhu

Caitlyn Zhu is a rising sixth grader, a writer, and a poet. When she's not writing, she loves to be in her garden. It's mostly a vegetable and herb garden because you get to eat them! Caitlyn hopes to write more stories about animals.

Tasslyn Magnusson: What changed when you revised? And how much changed?

Caitlyn Zhu: I changed the formatting to make more use of white space and to make the reader read the poem differently. The format changed, but only a few of the words changed. In formatting it was like everything changed! I learned new ideas about how to use white space and used this to change how the reader would read my poem.

Q: Did you think you'd change stuff?

A: I thought that we would change the formatting, but not as much as we did. I also thought that we might change a few words.

Q: When did you start writing?

A: I wrote for fun for the first time when I was in kindergarten.

Q: Why do you enjoy writing?

A: I like it because I can hide messages in my writing and I can express my ideas and try to change the world through it. Writing also lets all my ideas come out so I'm not daydreaming during math class.

Q: Where do you like to write?

A: I write in my room at my desk. I write only on the computer. It's faster and I can save and revise my work better. Information is also stored in a much smaller, portable space than if I wrote on paper.

Q: How do you come up with ideas?

A: Usually from other books or stories and my experiences or from something I care about deeply. I'm writing a second story that is half inspired by my garden and half inspired by *Wishtree*, which is written from the perspective of a tree.

Q: What do you like to do when you're not writing?

A: I like going on hikes but not the eleven mile kind. I like gardening and playing tennis. I plant a vegetable garden every year. Vegetable gardens are more useful than flower gardens because we get to harvest and eat the vegetables. Plus, most vegetable plants also flower!

Q: What are your favorite books to read?

A: Fantasy—crossed with historical fiction plots with lots of adventure. My favorites are always from the perspectives of animals or from people close to animals.

My Life In A Paper Bag

by

Caitlyn Zhu

If my life had to be described by
five items
in
a paper bag, it would

contain…
A peach, the
drops
of
juice
as clear and sweet as
golden
glass
beads,
the taste unable to leave my mouth
after
it
is
gone.

A pencil, the
lead
worn
D
O
W
N
from countless ideas
rubbed
onto
paper,
eraser worn to the metal band
at
the
end
from rubbing mistakes off of
a heap of thoughts etched onto a snowy white sheet.

Rustling in the bag would be a paintbrush,
the tuft of soft hair
at
the
end
unfurling blossoms of colors bright as a
rainbow,
forming
flowers,
forming the bird singing in a tree,
forming a fish swimming
in a blue ocean with
kelp
twirling
in
a circle of green,

creating things that
don't
even
exist.

Tiny black eyes
and a blue
and white body peek
out
of
my bag.
He is a penguin, and he is real.
Although everyone says that he
is only a
bundle of cotton
and cloth
and thread,
I still see
the flash of life in
those
eyes.

The paper crackles
as I turn the pages of
a book.
Each word is a drop, each sentence a ripple
A river
A lake
A sea
A stream
These waters absorb me,
make me see light and motion,
make me feel
sorrow
and joy.

I can run through
The swamps,
forests,
and rivers of fire
Feel for the
animals
and
humans
on their quests.
It is so much more than
a stack of paper under
a cover.
There is a whole new world

under that cover…

And another world
in that bag.

Building Conflict

Julia Hettiger asked Vedant Balan to build conflict during the revision process through imagining what might happen if his characters failed in his story, *Free Solo*.

Dear Reader,

When reading books, we often find ourselves on the edges of our seats wondering whether or not our favorite characters are going to make it out of sticky situations. These spine-tingling moments are possible because our favorite authors aren't afraid to make their characters fail, to put them in situations that seem impossible to escape. That's exactly what Vedant worked on when revising his short story, *Free Solo*.

Free Solo follows Joey and his two siblings as they face obstacles in order to reach their goal of finding a legendary mine filled with gold. At its heart, *Free Solo* is an adventure story, filled with twists and turns. And it was these twists and turns that Vedant worked on in his revision process.

I tasked Vedant with asking himself what would happen if his characters failed. While there were plenty of obstacles throughout the story, he worked on expanding them and figuring out what would happen should the characters fail to overcome them at first.

In his revisions, Vedant focused on key points in the story, ones that at first went by too quickly, and worked to slow them down. He did this in order to increase the tension in these scenes to keep his readers at the edges of their seats.

He also let his characters fail. Sometimes, as writers, we're hesitant to do this because we don't want to be mean to our characters or to see them in situations that could hurt them. But you'll find that as you write scenes like these, the harder it is to get out of certain situations, the bigger the payoff will be and the greater the lesson learned for your characters and often your readers, too.

Whether you're writing adventure or fantasy, science fiction or contemporary stories, good scenes are important, especially the ones that seem to throw our characters off track of doing what they need to do in order to accomplish their goals. Don't be afraid to let your characters fail or to put them in situations that seem impossible to escape. Doing what Vedant did in his revisions can help to make your story a wild roller coaster ride that readers are sure to love.

Happy Writing!

Julia Hettiger

Julia Hettiger is a writer from El Paso, Texas. By day, she works in higher education and marketing and by night, she writes stories full of magic and friendship for children. She has a marketing degree from The University of Texas at El Paso and is currently going for her MFA in Writing for Children and Young Adults at Hamline University.

Vedant Balan

Vedant Balan lives in Seattle, Washington. He is eleven years old, and attends Woodinville Montessori School. He is in fifth grade and likes math, science, and creative writing. He has a four-year-old brother and no pets. He loves to read fantasy novels and play with Legos. He plays tennis, and skis during the winter.

Julia Hettiger: What changed when you revised for building conflict?

Vedant Balan: I feel like my story got a bit longer. I added some more dialogue, too. And I learned, like you explained to me, it's okay to make your characters fail. So, in the new version I sent you, at the part when they're by the river, Joey tries to actually swim at first, but he can't do it. So then, he finds out that he can climb the slope and jump.

Q: When did you start writing?

A: I've always liked creative writing. I feel like I wrote my first story almost in, like, preschool. Then, in kindergarten, I don't know if you've heard of the book, *If You Give a Mouse a Cookie*. I made a different version of that book called, *If You Give a Rabbit a Habit*.

Q: How do you come up with your ideas?

A: For this story, I was thinking about the world we live in, but where electricity is extinct. I was just thinking about how phones and electronics are becoming a part of everyday life, like we're kind of being consumed by them. So, I just wanted to have a world where those things don't exist anymore and see how life would shape out. And then the gold mine idea, I've always liked scavenger hunts and I feel like this story is something like a hunt. Then, I thought of putting obstacles along the way as the characters are getting closer and closer to finding the gold. Then, all of a sudden, they have a giant wall that's in front of the mine.

Q: What are some of your favorite books? Would you say they impacted this story?

A: My favorite book right now is called *The Crossover*. I also like this book, it was a Newbery honor winner, called *The Evolution of Calpurnia Tate*. It's about this girl who, she lives in 1899, in Texas, and she's really interested in science. And she and her grandfather, they collect specimens out by the river. She has six brothers and her mother wants her to be a proper housewife, like learn to knit and cook but she absolutely hates knitting and cooking, so yeah.

Q: What advice would you give to other young writers who might not like the revision process?

A:

Dear Fellow Young Writers,

If you are a young writer that doesn't enjoy the revision process, I have been where you are. You may not like hearing so many negatives about your story. I have some advice for you. Your editor is only trying to make you story the best it can be. There is nothing wrong with making changes. You will make lots of amends and changes in your life. Editing and revision are just part of the story-writing process you will need to make your story the finest it can be. I hope that after reading this you feel more comfortable with having someone edit your story. If not, then keep working towards that goal.

Yours Truly,

Vedant

Free Solo

by

Vedant Balan

I was riding my bike down an alley in the marketplace with dumpsters and litter everywhere when I heard the revving of the steamcycle following me. I pedaled as fast as I could, but the steamcycle caught up to me in a matter of seconds. I was shoved against the wall and I felt an object pushed against the small of my back. When I dared to look down, I saw that the hand holding the object was not one of flesh, but a brass and silver clockwork prosthetic with gears and cogs. Many people who could afford it, replaced lost limbs with clockworks, and most of them were Explorers. Explorers, like my deceased father, were the people that went out looking for new lands, and they often lost arms and legs on their treacherous journeys.

Then, the man spoke. He had the arrogant, gruff voice that most Explorers had used at that time.

The words that came out were, "Look down."

I looked and saw him holding not a weapon of any kind, but

rather a sort of package about as big as my head.

"You must be Jonathan," he said.

How did he know my name?

"Yes, that's my name, but everyone calls me Joey," I replied uneasily.

"I knew your father" he smiled. "This is from him."

He shook the package. I kept my hand by my side where it was. The man's smile faltered.

"How do you happen to know my father?" I asked. "Can you tell me his name, favorite color, and favorite trail?"

"I can understand you are suspicious, with the way things happen these days," he replied. "My name is Samuel Watkins. I met your father shortly before his death. His name? Tim, Timothy Jason Jenkins. His favorite color was crimson, and his favorite trail was Cougar Cliff."

My anxiety dissipated entirely. This man had no way of getting around my father's alibi name, Jimmy Edwards, his false favorite color, gold, and his usage of his second-favorite trail, Rattlesnake Ledge. My father was always careful around his identity when he met someone new. To tell someone all three things truthfully, he would have to deeply trust them. This man was someone my father knew and trusted.

I took the package and mounted my bike. I nodded to the man, and pedaled away on my bike. During my trip home, I saw an antique shop's window display with maps from the 2000's. I dismounted my bike and ran in. I looked all around me and saw all the old, yellowing sheets. It was still hard for me to believe that at some they point in time they believed that there were only seven continents. I hopped back on my bike and rode to our house.

Rodeo Island was basically a heap of rocks dumped into the ocean off the coast of New York City by the government in an elaborate fashion. It was made mostly as a hotel for Explorers of the world who were passing by, but the island had a few residents. In this solemn year of 3024, most of the houses were just crumbling wrecks that nobody lived in anymore. I walked over to the house that now belonged to me and my siblings. I dropped off the bread I'd grabbed and headed into the old bomb shelter. I locked the hatch behind me and descended down the ladder into the metal bunker. I greeted Pucci, our parrot.

He replied, his voice echoing around the chamber, "Bread, Bread, Bread for Pucci. I saw great things today, no?"

Pucci was a Black Knight parrot, and he got on my nerves sometimes. I unclasped him from his perch, and he took flight happily.

I jumped down the stairs, and heard my brother, Jack, discussing some old maps with CJ, who was my sister. Jack was a broad shouldered teenager, and he was always being told that he looked exactly like my father. I was on the skinny side, and it sometimes annoyed me. CJ was a year younger than me, and she was the most hyper person I knew. I guess that came from her love of skydiving. She had dark brown hair, and deep blue eyes like me and our mother. Our mom had died when I was three, and none of us remembered much about her. I ran over and told them in full detail about the man with the clockwork hand. Jack asked me where the package was, so I pulled it out. We tore the paper together, and it revealed a large leather-bound book. Not only that, but the book was compressing a thin sheet of leather. We pulled out the leather sheet and saw that

there was writing on it. The sheet was a map.

"How come there's only half of a map?" CJ asked.

I looked and saw she was right, the map looked as if it was missing a large piece.

"Maybe Dad didn't get to the end of the map," Jack suggested.

He was probably right.

At that moment, Pucci perked up. "Steamcycles in the driveway! Pucci knows all."

I glanced out the window and saw the steam powered motorbikes parked outside.

"Hide the map!" Jack shouted.

I shoved it into the refrigerator. Moments later, there was a knock at the door.

We opened the door and a man and a woman stepped in. The woman had a clockwork eye, so I assumed she must have lost the real one. Both had the NAFD agent logo printed in bright red on their camouflage uniforms. NAFD stood for National Association for Discovery. They were the government department that oversaw all Explorers looking for new lands. They asked me if I had seen any men with clockwork hands, and a chill ran down my spine. I looked at my siblings, and they both shook their heads slightly.

I told the agents, "I don't think I did."

The woman pushed further, "Are you sure, we have reliable sources that tell us he might have known your father."

I told them I was sure, and they left the bunker.

"Do you think that was about the map?" Jack asked.

"Probably, why else would they talk about the man with the clockwork hand?" I replied.

"We should ask one of dad's fellow Explorers," said CJ.

We all thought that was a good idea, so we packed our bags and set off.

Mike Phillips was one of my father's fellow Explorers, and he lived on Rodeo Island near us, so we decided to pay him a visit.

When we got there, we knocked on the mahogany door.

A gruff voice answered, "Come in."

We opened the door, and found Mr. Phillips sitting at his desk with some coffee and newspapers. I sat down across from him and laid out the map. His eyes darted to it immediately. We sat like that for a couple of minutes. Suddenly, he shot out his hand and snatched the map. He dashed out of the room and up a flight of stairs. CJ, Jack, and I chased after him. We found Phillips in what used to be a nursery. We made our way through the mess of bottles and toys to where he was standing in the corner. He made a wild sprint for the door, but Jack immediately moved to block him. CJ pinned him to the wall while I fished the map out of his leather vest. I stuffed the paper back into my pocket and turned my attention back to the culprit.

"You seem to know a lot about this map. We might just let you go if you tell us what it leads to," I said.

"Deal," he growled. "I'll tell you about the legend of Dan Foley's mine," he began. "A long time ago, a man named Dan Foley was visiting Arizona. Apparently, he came across a large hole in the ground. When he went underground, he saw gold everywhere. He was amazed by his find, and he was just making plans for how he would spend the money when a terrible earthquake hit. That earthquake registered 6.7 on the Richter scale, and it brought up

some of the most fantastic cliffs in the area. Mr. Foley couldn't make it out of the mine and he never got to strike it rich. Tales of the old mine have gone around for decades, but no one knows where it is. Except maybe a skilled cartographer that was your father."

My siblings and I were awed. We released Mr. Phillips and hauled him down the stairs. Suddenly, we heard the wail of sirens.

"Darn it!" I exclaimed.

Phillips must have raised the alarm somehow, and now we were stuck. If we told them that Mr. Phillips was the real criminal, they would ask us to explain the story with detail. We couldn't do that without bringing up the map, which they'd definitely confiscate.

I turned to Mr. Phillips and started talking, "You stay here. When the police come in, you are going to tell them you were robbed, and that the robbers ran out the back door. Got it?"

He nodded weakly. We left him on the stairs, and silently made our way out. Finally, we made it out the door, but it was too late. The cars had encircled the house, so they would easily see through the lie that Phillips would tell them. The only way out was going to get us in deep trouble.

I nodded to CJ, and her eyes lit up.

I yelled, "Go!"

CJ jumped on top of a police car, and found a way inside. She pushed the startled policeman out through the door and motioned to us to join her. We ran into the car, and she stepped on the gas.

"We're fugitives now," she said, with a gleam in her eyes.

"Is that a good thing?" yelled Jack.

After some time, we came to a forest. We left the car at the edge and walked on foot. CJ took the lead, and Jack and I followed her. We came to a clearing, where we sat down to rest.

"Were you allowed to drive that car?" I asked CJ.

"Nope," she replied, without looking back.

That night, we unrolled our sleeping bags and crashed in a trench. I fell into a fitful sleep full of dreams about snakes and scorpions in the desert. I imagined us as the richest people in the world. Then I imagined us getting lost in the desert and never finding our way back.

When we woke up in the morning, we agreed unanimously to pool all the money we had brought to pay for a trip to Arizona, which was the general location of the map. We dug through the rucksacks and backpacks we had packed and found a total of three hundred ninety seven dollars. In the morning, we went to NAFD's airport and scheduled a hot air balloon flight for 4:30 p.m. It was still eleven in the morning, so we spent the day at the airport.

"How much money do we have left?" asked CJ.

I looked and saw that we had fifty-nine dollars left.

"Why do you ask?" I replied.

"There's a fast food restaurant right there" she said, pointing across the hallway.

I followed her gaze and my eyes found the blinking sign of Six Men Burgers and Fries. I thought that fifty-nine dollars would be enough for burgers and fries.

"We can go inside, but lets keep a low profile. The authorities might be looking for us after that incident," said Jack.

In the restaurant, we saw a soda dispenser and the large gears and cogs that worked it. We all agreed that the soda would satisfy us more than any real food, so I ordered three root beers. As

we sipped away, we discussed the history of Mack Machines. Mack Machines were operated by something called electricity, which was used back in the 21st century. Mack Machines became such a part of everyday life that people started trusting them too much. Criminals and hackers saw this as an opportunity, and they found a way to hack the machines and cause global chaos. Because of this, by 2098, electricity was extinct. After that, people returned to clockworks and steam-powered vehicles. They were less reliable and modern, but much safer.

After we were relaxed and full, we saw the time. It was 4:27. We hurried to where our balloon waited on the air field, and climbed in. The driver pulled a lever, and we shot into the air. I felt the cool wind against my face, and I felt compelled to whistle out loud.

Eventually, CJ fell asleep. I didn't even know it was possible to fall asleep on a hot air balloon, but my sister could do amazing things. After an hour, the vast desert of Arizona came into view. Everywhere I looked, there was deep green cacti and rolling dunes. The whole time we were on the balloon, Pucci was flying behind us, so when we landed he dove straight for the comfort of the sand on the ground, and fell into a deep snooze. We paid our driver and ran in the direction the map indicated. After some time, I remembered something Dad had taught us a long time ago.

"Guys! Let's go sandboarding!" I yelled.

"Oh yeah!" CJ replied.

We found some old wood, and fashioned teardrop shaped sheets out of them with our pocket knives. I ran up to the top of a dune and balanced myself onto the board. I jerked the board forward and sped down the hill.

"Woohoo," I yelled.

Jack and CJ followed my lead, and we made good time. I wasn't exactly looking around and my board crashed into something hard. I flew into the sand and scraped my knees.

"What was that?" I exclaimed.

It looked like a sort of car roof. Then I saw the red NAFD logo on it.

"Look at this, guys!" I called.

Jack and CJ ran up a large sand dune to me.

"It looks like a Steambuggy!" Jack yelled. We started digging frantically, and we found a large, grey, dune buggy-like vehicle.

"Do you think it still works?" asked CJ.

"Probably," I replied. "Those were tested and they survived a 3,000 feet tall sequoia tree being dropped on them."

"Dad taught me how to drive one of these when I was fourteen," said Jack.

We all got in and Jack started driving us the way the map indicated. I was in the front passenger seat, and I felt around in the storage compartments. It seemed like it was made from leather. I pulled it out and froze.

"Guys! I found the other part of the map!" I yelled.

Jack stomped on the brakes, making us all lurch forward. He handed me the part we already had and the pieces fit together perfectly. The new piece had one symbol I didn't understand. It seemed to be a sort of wall.

After a while, we came to a river. This was good news, because it meant we were following the map correctly. The bad news was that the buggy couldn't make it across. It looked like we were going to

finish the journey on foot. The other bad news was that I couldn't swim. As toddlers, Jack and CJ had mastered the technique, but I was always wary of the water. CJ spotted this problem, and we thought for a while. I decided there was no way but to try to swim. I went first, taking a deep breath and plunging into the water. Even in the first few seconds, I knew something was wrong. I flailed and thrashed wildly, trying to breathe. I felt two sets of hands on my back, and Jack and CJ pulled me out.

"That didn't work," I said.

Eventually, I remembered my talents, which were rock climbing and rope-swinging. I looked around and saw a cliff with a thick vine that looked like it could support my weight. While my siblings swam across, I scaled the mighty rock. Eventually, I reached the top, my hands bruised and stomach cramped. I stared at the swirling water below. It had to be at least ten feet deep. If I fell in, I was sure to drown. I grabbed the thick vine and jumped off. I timed my release well, and flew into the air. I landed in a tree's branches, and I scrambled down quickly. Little did I know that this was only a taste of what would come to be.

Pretty soon, we came to a dense, green, forest. We entered the woods and saw the sun-dappled leaves casting dark shadows onto the ground.

"According to the map, we're getting close to the mine. There's some sort of yellow wall symbol drawn in front of the mine," said CJ.

"Can we get around it?" asked Jack.

"No, it says on the bottom of the map that we can't get to it any other way. I think it's surrounded by dense cacti," she replied.

"We'll find out what it is when we get there," I told them.

We found a clearing to set up a camp for the night. We pitched the bright yellow tents and laid out our sleeping bags. CJ and I went into the forest with Pucci to look for firewood. We grabbed a nice stack of thick, dry birch wood and headed back to the campsite.

"Aiiii! Me sleepy," were Pucci's last words before he dove into his miniature sleeping bag.

We all climbed into our sleeping bags and eventually fell asleep.

In the morning, we all got up and folded the tent quickly. Our goal was to get to the mine that day. We ran as fast as we could, and suddenly, Jack was buried in yellow sand.

"Quicksand!" I yelled.

"Don't panic, Jack!" CJ shouted.

We wasted a good five seconds getting over our shock.

"The fishing pole!" I yelled.

We grabbed one of the fishing poles in Jack's backpack and held it out to him. He reached for it, and barely missed.

"No!" CJ exclaimed.

Jack's head went under. I couldn't think of what to do. There was only one, extremely dangerous way to save him. It could kill me.

"I'm going in," I told CJ. "Build a pulley and tie the end of the string to me. When I tug twice, pull us out."

She nodded.

"Use these to keep the sand out of your eyes," she said, handing me her lab goggles.

I put them on, took a deep breath, and jumped under. All I saw was yellow grains of sand. My eyes wouldn't be able to help me find Jack. I put out my hands, hoping to feel his arms. After a minute

or so, I felt Jack's hand. I grabbed it and pulled on the rope twice. After a few seconds, we were back on dry land. I set Jack down in the shade. He was breathing, but he was unconscious. After some time, he came to. He leaned against a tree and coughed up a lot of sand.

"Thanks," he said weakly.

We sat there resting for some time, and then started moving again. After a few more hours of running and hiking, we came to the spot where the mine was located on the map. I looked up, and at that moment I understood what the wall on the map meant.

"Whoa" said Jack and CJ in unison.

We were staring up at an enormous stone cliff about six hundred feet tall. There was a glint of gold on the other side that could be seen through dense cacti. There were foot-long spikes on the already abnormally tall cacti.

"Joey," CJ said. "That free soloing you did at the river a few days ago might come in handy right about now."

"All right, I'll do it, but let's make a parachute, in case I slip," I decided.

They agreed, so Jack brought out what was left of our tents, and CJ used some fishing line. Together, they made a parachute that looked as if it might work. They fastened it to CJ's skydiver pack, and I started my ascent. It was a difficult climb.

By the time I reached the top, I was ready to take a nap. Then I saw that the cliff really was like a wall. There was still the other side of the cliff to climb down. I was so angry and frustrated, I almost didn't see CJ waving her arms. Once she saw that she had my attention, she started pointing to her back. My parachute! I crouched down low, and leaped into the air. I timed it carefully and pulled the rip cord as hard as I could. My chute popped out behind me, and I sailed to the ground. I spotted the hole in the ground and descended carefully.

The rough dirt walls were the first thing I saw. Then I noticed a rusted steel axe on the ground. I hefted it up and put it into my parachute bag. I head rats rustling through the debris, and I spotted some lizard skeletons too. The place gave me the creeps.

The main door was fastened shut, and I tried pushing it. It wouldn't budge. I hefted my axe and chopped through the door What I saw next amazed me. Piles three meters high of dusty gold bars were everywhere. There were mine carts on broken rails full of gold coins. I ran outside and cut through the cacti with my axe. I looked around, and spotted Jack and CJ near the forest.

"Did you find anything?" they asked at the same time.

"That place is loaded with money. Phillips wasn't lying," I told them.

While I was gone, Jack and CJ had found another yellowing NAFD Steambuggy. We hopped in, and Jack drove us into the mine. We piled in as much gold and money as possible. We made three trips like that, and eventually we came back to the river where we had ditched the first buggy. The current had slowed down, and Jack was able to drive it across. We roped the two together, and that way, we were able to carry all the gold back to the airport. When we got there, our balloon driver saw us, and his jaw hit the ground.

"Well, you found the treasure of Dan Foley's mine. What are you going to do with it?"

"We're going to give half of it to farmers and other people who grow crops like wheat and corn. We hope that once we do that, it will end all food shortages of bread and vegetables going on right

now," replied Jack.

I thought that was a good idea, and I added, "Of course, we're still going to have a lot of money, so we can move into a really nice house and live a luxurious life."

Everyone laughed at that. We got in, and the balloon surprised me by taking the full weight of all the gold we had. Once we got back to NAFD's airport in New York City, a huge crowd of government agents swarmed us. Once they saw that we had the gold, they backed off. We could hire the best lawyer in town with the money we had if they tried us in court. We were then hit by another swarm, this time of New York newspaper reporters. After what seemed like an eternity, we were able to get back to our modest house on Rodeo Island, we sat down in our couch chairs.

"That journey might have made us the richest people in the world, but it was more the adventure and fun that I enjoyed," CJ told us.

I couldn't agree more.

Setting for Complications

Ailynn Collins mentored Liana Zhu through revisions of her story, *Amelia Furhart–A Story of a Cat's Determination*, focused on creating tension through setting.

Dear Reader,

When writing a story, it's important to create tension and keep that up to the end. The reader will root for the character, hoping that they'll overcome the obstacles set in their way. This tension is what keeps the reader reading.

Sometimes tension can be created by the plot becoming more and more difficult, scary, or horrid for the character. Sometimes, a character's weakness can get it the way of their success. And sometimes, as in this story, the setting can create obstacles for the character.

Our revision focus for *Amelia Furhart* was **Setting for Complication**.

Setting is important to every story, as it puts the reader in the world of the characters. We, as readers, get to experience the sights, sounds, smells, and feeling of the places the character encounters.

Every main character should have a desire, a goal. For Amelia, it was not only to fly, but to get into the plane's cockpit. Sometimes, it is the antagonist who does all they can to get in the way of the main character's desires. This creates tension.

In this story, there's no character who is an antagonist. So, the setting—the obstacles—become the antagonist. Amelia needs to face all kinds of problems to get to her dream place. The writer would want readers to root for the cat, and hope that she gets what she wants. When she overcomes her difficulties, and achieves her goals, readers will cheer.

This is where Liana used the setting (the airplane and its layout, and even the passengers) to create this complication, making it hard for Amelia to get what she wants.

How did she put obstacles in Amelia's way, so that there was tension in the story? First, she added sensory details. When Amelia got on board the plane, we thought about what the cat would experience in terms of smell, sights, sounds, and even the feel of the flooring under her paws. Cats are highly sensitive to their environment. Liana was able to give readers insight into a cat's world.

Next, when the passengers arrived and the plane took off, we looked at how that changed Amelia's experience. Did she get scared? What kept her from giving up and curling up into a corner, hoping the flight would end soon? Could her curiosity and determination to be like her ancestor overcome her fear?

Finally, Liana had to make it physically and emotionally difficult for Amelia to get from her hiding place to the pilot's cockpit. This is where the tension of the story began to build. We discussed how to do create difficulty. Maybe bags could be dropped, high heels could almost catch Amelia, loud talking would make her think she's been discovered. The idea that someone might see her before she reaches the cockpit and ends her dream, could be the big obstacle that has readers chewing their nails!

So, the next time you write a story, think about how you could use the setting to create tension. Obstacles, weather, and even the special sensitivities of the characters to their environment could be interesting ways to make things harder for them to reach their goals.

Happy writing,

Ailynn Collins

Ailynn Collins has been a Montessori teacher for many years and loves sharing her love of books and writing with her students. She has an MFA in Writing for Children and Young Adults from Hamline University. She is the author of several books for young and middle grade readers—mainly science fiction and nonfiction stories. When she's not writing, she is working with her five dogs on agility, obedience, and rally competitions. She is excited to join Young Inklings and share her love for writing with young authors everywhere.

Liana Zhu

Liana is in fourth grade at Living Wisdom School in California. She loves to read, draw, and play music, especially piano. She got the idea for this story while doing a report on Amelia Earhart. She had a cat picture on the top of her report and decided not to use it for her report. That's where she got the idea to write *Amelia Furhart—The Story of a Cat's Determination*.

Ailynn Collins: What do you like to write?
Liana Zhu: I started writing in first grade, in class. I used to like writing fictional stories about sea creatures. Now I like to write realistic fiction stories and adventure stories with animals.

Q: Why do you write?
A: Because I can express strong feelings about things—happiness, anger, sadness.

Q: Where do you like to write?
A: I usually write on my desk in the dining room, at the computer table. I also like to write in a faraway room, where there are no people.

Q: Do you like to discuss your stories with people?
A: I prefer to discuss the stories while I'm writing them. I talk to my writing teacher. I show my family my work. They really like the stories.

Q: What are you reading now?

A: I like to read fantasy stories. I'm reading the *Warrior* series. It's what inspires me to write animal stories.

Q: How did you come with the idea for this story?

A: I was writing a report about Amelia Earhart. There was a picture of a cat on top and I thought I could use this for Amelia Furhart, and she would be a cat.

Q: Do you ever feel blocked?

A: Yes!

Q: What do you do to get out of it?

A: Sometimes I take a break, go for a walk. Sometimes I type up the things I have so far in the story (which I haven't typed up yet) and I get new ideas.

Q: How did you feel about doing to the revision of Amelia Furhart?

A: At first, I didn't like it. Then when I actually read the story and realized I needed revision, then I liked it. The revision added more tension and I made more problems for my main character.

Amelia Furhart

A Story of a Cat's Determination

by

Liana Zhu

-Amelia Furhart V

Amelia Furhart was a sleek, stray tabby cat that lived in Half Moon Bay Airport. She slept in the lost baggage claim room of Gate 3, eating scraps under the tables of the food court.

Because it was such a small airport, only a few private planes flew in and out of here during the daytime. At night, Amelia was free to wander the halls and the tarmac.

In the outer hallway, there was an old black and white poster titled, *Amelia Earhart 1937*. Amelia Furhart loved this poster. It was a piece of her own history, as told by her mother when Amelia was just a kitten.

"Your great-great-great-great-great-grandmother met

Earhart," her mama used to say. "She took her aboard her plane, the Lockheed Electra. They had a great friendship. Your ancestor named one of her kittens Amelia. And so each generation of our family has had a female kitten named Amelia."

"Tell me the story again!"

"Earhart had a stopover here," Mama would say, stopping to clean her whiskers. "She needed to rest and refuel on her flight across the Pacific Ocean. As she disembarked, she almost stepped on great-great-great-great-great-grandmother who came to greet her on the tarmac! Earhart bonded with her immediately, and they shared breakfast and a nap together. She told her all about her flight, how exciting it was to fly like a bird. She even took her on board the Electra."

That night, Amelia was thinking about Great-great-great-great-great grandmother as she watched the gulls circling above the runway.

The gulls have those long flat forelegs, just like planes. But the gulls don't make noise. They are flapping those stretched out things riding on the wind. I bet I could do that!

She climbed onto the highest waiting area bench, then took a long, flying leap into the sky, paws outstretched.

Evelyn Whitby, the custodian, was sweeping the floors around Gate 3. She saw Amelia crash land.

She laughed, "You are a very silly cat. Cats aren't supposed to fly!"

Still, Amelia was not going to give up. After passing under Earhart's poster, and recalling her mama's story for the umpteenth time, Amelia made a bold decision.

Even if only once, I must fly in an airplane!
How could she make it happen?
She hatched a plan.
She would stow away on a plane.
But how could she get on board?

Late every night, Evelyn made her cleaning rounds. She cleaned the one or two airplanes that were parked there for the night. Amelia and Evelyn met each other often in the empty hallways. Evelyn was kind to her.

"Here Kitty, have the rest of my tuna sandwich," she'd say.

Evelyn's cleaning cart was stored in the lost baggage room. Amelia noticed how the lower cart shelves were only half loaded with toilet paper and supplies. Just enough room for a sleek small cat to hide inside!

So, after a hearty dinner of Food Court scraps, Amelia squeezed in between the paper towels on the cleaning cart. At 8:05 that night, Evelyn pushed the cart out of the baggage room, then up the ramp to the now empty Gulfstream Air Jet at Gate 1.

It was a bumpy ride. Amelia tucked her tail in, so as not to expose it. The overpowering smell of Lysol cleaner made her whiskers twitch. While Evelyn was humming a tune and cleaning the passenger seats, Amelia slinked fur-tively off the cleaning cart and into the snack galley just behind the pilot's cabin.

Right after the pilot is finished taking off, I will sneak into the cockpit and introduce myself. If I appear too early, they will just throw me off the plane!

After a lonely night's sleep in a galley cabinet, Amelia woke up, body stiff from sleeping on the hard floor. She was also very

thirsty, because she hadn't had any water since the night before. She saw a shaft of light filtering through the half open storage cabinet that she was in. She also heard passengers shuffling through the main cabin.

Amelia stretched. She smelled something that she had never smelled before in her whole cat life. It was quite different from the familiar fragrance of the lost baggage room in the Half Moon Bay airport. This smell was from all new suitcases.

She was about to leap out of the cabinet when she saw a flight attendant heading toward her. The flight attendant was coming closer! Before the flight attendant could see her, Amelia backed into the shadows of the cabinet. No one would see her here.

Then, she heard the crew talking, "Looks like we have 20 more minutes before takeoff."

Amelia took the time to give herself a good wash with her rough tongue, licking and rubbing with her paw, from whiskers to tail. It calmed her down. She felt drowsy and dozed off.

When she woke up, an announcement came over the intercom, "Good morning, ladies and gentlemen. We will be taking off soon. Please stow your tray tables, bring your seats upright and fasten your seat belts. Thank you and enjoy your short flight to Monterey Regional Airport."

And just like that, the plane took off, engines roaring.

Amelia prowled out of the cabinet and got ready to leap.

She heard a person exclaim, "Flight attendant, I'm having allergies. Is there cat hair somewhere in here?!"

"What are you talking about? There are no cats, or any crated animal in here. I'm sure!" While the flight attendant was talking, she fished around for a box of tissues.

While that was happening, Amelia stalked toward a fold-down chair that another flight attendant was sitting on. She ducked under it. Suddenly, a bag dropped from the overhead cabinet. It made a loud thud.

Amelia was so scared. She leaped into the nearest hiding place that she could reach. It turned out to be the pilot's cockpit. The door was slightly ajar, giving enough room for Amelia to squeeze into. The pilot was gripping the control wheel as the plane gained altitude. Now was her chance! She leaped onto the co-pilot seat.

"Meoww!" she introduced herself, feeling very nervous.

The pilot gasped, "How on earth did you get in here, Smart Kitty?!"

She gave him a slow blink, and lowered her tail in guilt as if to say, "I came in on a cleaning cart and stowed away!"

"I wish I had noticed you sooner," he continued. "I can't turn this plane around, so you'll have to fly with us to Monterey. You'll have to be my official co-pilot for this flight!"

Amelia winked at him and proceeded to give her paws a good lick. The pilot radioed ahead to the Monterey control tower.

"We have a stow-away cat on this flight! Please be prepared with an animal crate upon landing at Gate 6."

Amelia rubbed up against his arm, and then, for the first and only time of her cat life, settled down to watch the sky from the co-pilot's seat.

She saw an endless cloud-covered sky over a vast blue ocean. She imagined the clouds were gray and white mice scampering across a bare field. Once the captain had put the plane on autopilot, he rubbed Amelia's ears and pointed down at the water.

"Look Kitty, there's the Monterey Bay!"

Amelia saw two fish, tails raised, swimming in the ocean.

"You're probably thinking those are fish," said the pilot. "But those are really humpback whales, and they're much bigger than this plane!"

Amelia saw the bright sun, high in the sky, reflected on the blue-green ocean, with floating islands of seaweed. The water stretched as far as she could see. She knew at once that she loved the ocean.

Suddenly, the plane took a sharp dip and Amelia fell off her seat onto the cockpit floor.

"Don't worry, Kitty. It's only turbulence," the pilot assured her.

A few minutes later, a flight attendant poked her head into the cockpit and asked, "Would you like any drinks, Captain?"

The pilot answered, "A coffee for me please, a dish of milk for my co-pilot, and an airline's stuffed bear."

Amelia gratefully lapped up the milk. She was so parched after her stowaway night.

The flight attendant brought in a stuffed bear, a souvenir from *Skyways Airlines*. The captain removed the tiny pilot's cap. He turned to Amelia and said, "You have been an excellent mini co-pilot, so I'm awarding you with your very own captain's hat!"

As he strapped the hat onto Amelia's head, she imagined she had flown with the great Amelia Earhart. She felt so proud to be the First Cat Aviator.

"Flight attendants please be seated for arrival." the pilot announced over the intercom.

The plane landed at the Monterey Regional Airport in the early afternoon. Amelia watched as the dials on the instrument panel flashed back and forth. She batted at them as if they were mice. She pounced everywhere, searching for them.

The pilot howled with laughter. "Tricked you, Kitty!"

Minutes later, a crate was waiting for her on the tarmac. The captain and crew saluted her as her crate was loaded back onto the return flight to Half Moon Bay Airport.

"Thanks, Pilot," Amelia mewed. "I wish I could stay on your plane!"

That evening, as Evelyn returned to the lost baggage room to get the cleaning cart, she heard a meowing sound coming from a pile of baggage! She rummaged in the big pile of suitcases, following the meowing sound. There, she found a crate with big bold letters written across the top of it: "LIVE ANIMAL". She had to rub her eyes. When she heard the meow again, she knew it was her cat friend.

"Where have you been, and where did the pilot hat come from?" Evelyn asked.

"The pilot gave it to me! I flew with him, just like Amelia Earhart!" she meowed, trying to explain.

"You are a lucky stray cat to have been returned here," Evelyn cried, hugging Amelia tightly. "Promise me that you won't sneak away again."

Amelia rubbed her body against Evelyn, and purred, "I'm Amelia Furhart, named after Amelia Earhart! Just like Amelia Earhart said on her poster, *Adventure is worthwhile in itself*. So why shouldn't I have adventures too?"

And they strolled to the food court to share a tuna sandwich.

Pacing

Megan White guided Simon Chien in a revision focused on pacing to develop the road map of his story, *A Story of Nature*.

Dear Reader,

Finding the right pacing for your story can be tricky. As you're writing, ideas can come at you from all directions. It's easy to just throw everything in as you think of it and see where the story takes you. When you finish the story, though, this way of writing can leave your plot a little lost in all the directions it has taken.

The traditional structure of a story begins with exposition, goes to rising action, then the climax, the falling action, and the resolution. There's no right way to structure your story, and there are a hundred ways to mess with this structure to make the story what you want. However, usually this structure is a good road map to keep in mind to build the most tension and keep your readers excited the whole way through your story.

For Simon's story, we found that the amount of excitement and tension through every scene almost took away from the dramatic climax, the moment when the mysteries are revealed and the most intense action is happening. We brainstormed some ways to balance out all of the elements of the plot so that the reader would be able to keep up.

A good way to do this is to actually slow down your story sometimes. It can be a little overwhelming for the reader when there's constant action happening, and they never get a chance to breathe and really think about what's been happening. Simon went through his story and looked for places where he might add in a slower scene, whether it be to add some characterization or to let us get to know the setting a little more. With some moments like these, the tense action scenes seem more exciting because of the contrast!

Happy Writing,

Megan White

Megan White is a college student at Skidmore, in New York. She grew up writing, and is currently majoring in creative writing and is hoping to work in publishing someday. She has been a part of the Society of Young Inklings since she was seven years old! Her hobbies include hiking, reading, writing, and getting lost into the depths of Netflix.

Simon Chien

Simon is ten years old and lives in Seattle, Washington. He wrote this story based on his love of snakes, and wanted unique names that are rarely used for humans. He also wanted to write about how humans affect nature. Apart from writing, other things he enjoys are doing sports, playing piano, and reading.

Megan White: How much of your story did you change? Did it surprise you how much you changed, or how much you wanted to change?
Simon Chien: It's kind of surprising, but I've been warned that there's a lot of changing in the revising process.

Q: How did you go about changing those things? What steps did you take in your revisions?
A: Well, I got a lot of help from my parents, and it took a while. There were a lot of obstacles. We first made the changes on paper and then we switched it over to the computer.

Q: What was your favorite part of the revision, and what was your least favorite part?
A: Probably my favorite part of the revision was writing the new paragraphs that I added in, because it was like writing all new stuff. My least favorite part was probably when you have one thing, and you want to change it because you realize something new, and you have to read through the whole story and change it all the way through, which was a little frustrating.

Q: Do you have any advice for other young writers and people revising for the first time?

A: It's probably going to be frustrating for you, but you just have to keep going through it. And ask for help!

Q: Where do your ideas come from?

A: Well, when you're doing schoolwork, or writing as a school assignment, you start out with something that might not sound that great, but you can have stuff like really crazy characters and then you can change your story into something a lot better.

Q: What's the difference for you between writing for school and writing at home?

A: For school I get a little more intense, because I think I make up better stuff when I'm assigned to do it. Before this, I didn't really like writing, so I didn't really do it at home, but school definitely motivates me more!

A Story
of Nature

by
Simon Chien

PROLOGUE

Behind a magnificent conifer in the Great Greypine Forest, near the coast of Florida, many decades ago, only one human with the right code could open the entrance to a hidden tree house. This person was Neon Zeer. If you wished to break in, you had to be strong, quick, and agile, for in and below the great conifer tree, which was a special species known as the Greypine, there were lasers, traps, and more doorways to be unlocked.

PART I

Neon was eleven years old. She was quick, smart, and was always up for a challenge. Hiking through the wilderness, she was never without her snake, Flame. She had found him a long time ago in the very forest she was in right now. In fact, Flame was the very reason why she decided to live there; Neon could not resist being surrounded by the variety of wildlife in the Greypine Forest. She especially enjoyed living near the tallest of all the Greypines.

The tree was so well known, locals in and near the forest called it the Great Greypine. This was the main thing in the forest's (small) reputation. It towered above all the other pines. If you looked at it by air, you would see all the other pines below but they were dwarfed by the Great Greypine. Flame was a rare type of snake that are no longer living, for when humans first found the tall grey pines, many wanted to cut the forest down for lumber, but the government protected it. Even though it may not have looked pretty at the time, it was teeming with life.

Flame was more than just a snake. One-of-a-kind, he was more closely related to the snake's ancient ancestor, the Dragon. Although he did not have wings or legs, Flame and the Dragon had one feature in common: they both breathed fire. This was kind of a problem because they often accidently torched trees, and Neon would have to rush to get water before the fire burned everything down. One day, when Neon was fetching water to quench the flames that were threatening to engulf her sofa, she thought, *it would be nice to have a snake that was water breathing so I wouldn't have to do all this work.*

The next day, Neon and Flame were adventuring in the

Greypine Forest, when Neon saw movement in the trees. Flame got scared and torched a tree. Neon quickly rushed back to the bunker to get water, but by the time she got back with a tank full of water, the flames were already out, water vapor rising from the charred tree. As Neon and Flame returned home, she wondered what it was that had drenched the flames.

PART II

He slithered through the thick underbrush of the Forest, and thought about the events that had occurred that morning. He'd seen a girl with a strange snake who breathed fire and had set a tree alight. He knew he must do something or the fire would jump from tree to tree and set the whole forest ablaze, so he invited Wave, his own snake, to extinguish the flames, but keeping both their identities a secret. Once the girl and her snake had gone from the forest, he quickly turned back into human form and motioned to Wave to return home.

PART III

That night Neon, just couldn't get the scene out of her mind, which was full of questions. What was it that extinguished the flames? Was it an animal or a human, and if it was an animal, then was it a new undiscovered species? Where was it now? She knew she must answer all these questions or she would never come to rest. The next day, she searched through the forest, which was no easy task. The forest, at the time, was the fifth largest in America, and the largest in Florida. Neon

searched and searched until sunset, not really knowing what she was looking for, and then finally went home. The thing, whatever it was, had left barely a trace.

PART IV

Curled around a tree, alongside Wave, he looked down. There below him was the illegal tree-cutting group S.L.D. (Supreme Lumber Delivery). They were unloading equipment from their van, which looked like a mad science research truck. (Clearly, they weren't very talented artists). He watched closely, until one worker with a chain saw was right under him. Without prompting, Wave spewed water all over the lumber worker in disapproval. The drenched man looked upward with a grimace, searching for the source of the water but saw nothing and went back to work. Although Wave had been helpful, he had to do something more drastic to stop them, but it was a large organization. Once the workers started chopping, odds were they would not stop until a good amount of the forest was down to stumps. The government was unreliable because they thought the Greypine Forest wasn't a very pretty piece of land, so they just assumed that after warning the public to not interfere with it, humans would back off, but they were wrong.

PART V

The next day, Neon searched again for the unknown thing or person that had drenched the flames with no luck. However, she did find the illegal lumber company that claimed to be a scientific research team, which was a pretty sorry lie, considering their sawing equipment. She listened to them talk. One worker seemed a bit wet and claimed water had just fallen from the sky. The other workers were all a bit amused by this statement. Perhaps it was the same thing that had extinguished the flames before? Neon snuck a peek into the lumber van it was full of tree chopping supplies.

At least we know what we're up against, Neon thought, as she drew back to the shadows of the trees.

PART VI

Neon had been searching for hours in all the books she had, but found no result for water-spewing animals.

Duh, she thought. *What kind of animal shoots waters out of its mouth? If there aren't any animals, then it must have been a human who had a bucket of water or a hose, but if it was a hose, then where would he or she get the water?*

She also wondered about the lumber company. *What would happen to all the animals? Would they be spared?* Neon knew she must act.

PART VII

As Neon went back to the tree house with Flame, she pondered how to stop the lumber company. She thought hard but could not come up with any ideas.

Slow down, she told herself, *you need a quiet place to think.*

She decided to go out again after checking and double

checking that the tree house door was locked, she went hiking in the woods, but it wasn't long before she heard footsteps in the woods.

PART VIII

He went back to his temporary campsite, lit a match that he used to light the kindling, and he sat down and thought. One idea kept coming up: *Sabotage the lumber truck as the workers were away. Maybe at lunch?*

He then collected a zipline and started toward a large Douglas fir. He climbed up it and shot the grappling hook to the tree, grabbed the zipline and zoomed down.

PART IX

While the S.L.D. workers were out on lunch break, he shifted to snake form and slithered through the open van window unnoticed. He loved being in snake form, but in order to investigate, he had to change back to human form. While searching through the supplies, he found five chain saws and two axes. He quickly bundled the lot, opened the back door of the van, and made a break for it. At that moment, a lone worker, who had left his water bottle in the van, had just spotted him and was running for help. Meanwhile, he sprinted into the trees.

He considered dropping the supplies, turning into a snake and slithering away, but he dismissed that idea.

No, he thought, *I have a mission.*

He kept on running and saw a girl. Soon, he realized she was the same girl with the fire-breathing snake as he had seen before, ahead.

The girl told him, "Go to the Great Greypine! Once there, you will see a damp spot on the ground. It will be right in front of the Great Greypine!"

"How do I know I can trust you?" he yelled back.

"You don't have a choice!" the girl replied, pointing at the workers who were gaining fast.

The girl vanished into the trees. Meanwhile, he tried to lose the workers before quickly reaching the meeting spot.

Uh oh, he thought when the workers came closer. He was cornered.

Just then he saw movement from the corner of his eye, the girl was back! She was spreading leaves on the ground.

"What are you doing?" he yelled.

The girl put a finger to her lips and her snake blew fire on the leaves creating a barricade between the angry workers and the two boys.

"Come on, this way," said the girl.

He followed.

PART X

Neon had seen the boy run swiftly through the trees, his arms full of chopping supplies. A few yards back were five angry workers from SLD!

I must help him but how?

And at that moment an idea came to mind. Flame would make a barricade of fire, allowing her and the other boy to escape. To make the fire last long enough, he would need something flammable and easy to get: leaves!

Yes, that would be perfect! she thought. *But just in case, I should water the spot so the flames don't get to us.*

As the boy came closer, she quickly informed the other boy of all her plans and hoped he would listen. She went to the Great Grey Pine and set the props.

Soon the boy came, heavily pursued by lumber workers. Neon started spreading the leaves in a semi-circle with The Great Grey Pine behind. When the boy got in the circle, Neon instructed Flame to set the leaves alight.

This better work, she thought.

They were cornered!

Flame set the leaves alight and, a blaze of orange and red light lit the forest. The flames started high but swiftly declined.

"Come on. This way!" she said.

He plunged into the forest hoping the other boy would follow. The boy did.

PART XI

Neon led the boy up to her tree house. Once there, he introduced himself as Indigo a shape-shifter whom had gotten his powers from spending so much time with his snake, Wave.

"So, it was you that extinguished the flames and drenched the worker!" Neon exclaimed.

Indigo hesitated for a moment and then slowly nodded. Neon gazed out the window and saw a snowflake drift to the ground, one thing was for certain: winter had begun.

EPILOGUE

The story goes on with more adventures to come. Together, Neon and Indigo are twice as strong, and ready to meet the next challenges to face them.

Interior Monologue

Malar Ganapathiappan mentored Maia Goel on a revision focused on developing character's interior monologue to build to heighten tension in Maia's story, *Whisperers*.

Dear Reader,

Internal monologue is the character's inner voice. It is a way to show the reader the character's thoughts, emotions, sensations and beliefs. In Maia's riveting story, Ivy's perspective brings the reader along for her adventure. It allows the reader to understand how she relates to the world and how her experiences affect her.

Maia and I focused on developing Ivy's internal monologue to build tension throughout *Whisperers,* while also making Ivy's character more real and relatable. Maia took a few steps to use internal monologue to develop the main themes in the story around Ivy's ambivalence towards her powers and her jealousy of her brother.

Maia first brainstormed the history of the Stear siblings. She answered questions like: "Where did she get her beliefs around the extent of her powers? How might she have initially learned about her abilities? Why is being a supportive older sister important to her? Questions like these around the important themes (like the origin of Ivy's ambivalence and jealousy, her motivation, and the dynamic between her and Owen) informed how she reacted to her experiences. Ivy is a supportive older sister, and also a girl blossoming into her powers and abilities. Maia played up this internal struggle by depicting the layers of her jealous thoughts and emotions.

When you're revising your own story, tune into the character's inner voice and observe what this is revealing about the character. Consider any important themes which might play a role in defining the character's experience. Consciously choose how the character responds to each situation based on their personality. Finally, highlight important details by taking out any information which doesn't serve the purpose of the plot. Subtle changes to the character's reactions to their experiences can add depth and make a significant difference.

Happy writing,

Malar Ganapathiappan

Malar Ganapathiappan is a writing mentor and coach. She enjoys guiding her clients to connect to their inner truth and find their fullest creative expression. She holds a bachelor's degree in Psychology and is a member of the Society of Children's Book Writers and Illustrators. When not reading or writing, she enjoys nature, fitness, art, and cats. You can find her online at malarganapathiappan.com.

Maia Goel

Maia Goel is a ninth grader at Menlo-Atherton High School, and this is her third year entering the Inklings Contest. She loves singing, dancing, and reading (especially fantasy fiction), and she wants to be a scientist. She loves to read and write about supernatural powers, which inspired her to write, *Whisperers*.

Malar Ganapathiappan: How did you get the idea for this story?

Maia Goel: My story started completely different. The idea first came from a book I read where the characters could talk to different elements. At some point, my story had dragons in it. Then I changed it completely to being set in the school year. Instead of it being a big problem they had to solve, it became more emotional. There isn't a lot of action in the story but it's about her coming to terms with it being about her brother. I would keep getting new ideas, try to fit them in, have them not work, and get a new idea. It kind of went all over the place.

Q: How do you typically come up with your ideas?

A: They just come to me. If I sit down and try to brainstorm ideas, those are usually not the ones I end up choosing to write about. The first time I wrote a long story was in 7th grade when I was doing an Inklings story. That idea came to me when I was walking down the street. I kept thinking about it over and over again and I came home and wanted to write it down. Because I found the story so interesting, I kept thinking about it and that's how it developed. Usually they come to me at moments when I'm not trying to come up with ideas.

Q: How did your story change after your revisions for internal monologue?

A: I replaced Ivy saying, "I'm feeling jealous" or "I don't know how I feel" with "tightness in my chest." I had Jack say, "you seem scared" for her to realize that she was scared. Adding the story of having to be a good sister helped. And saying "I have to stop feeling these feelings" showed more of her character. It showed how she wanted to do well and explained her jealousy.

Q: What advice do you have for other Young Inklings who don't like revision very much?

A: You can keep the main part of the story. Changing small things and putting in small things like sentences saying "I have to be a good sister," made a big difference. It didn't take me that long to put in those sentences. As soon as I started, I started getting more ideas. The hardest part is actually writing the story. Once you have it written down, you have it written down and you know what you have to do to make it better.

Whisperers

by

Maia Goel

The world is a strange and wonderful place. I'm a plant whisperer, which, as far as the known powers go, is pretty boring. Sure, I always know what plants around me need and, if I concentrate hard enough, I can even help them grow, but that's pretty much the extent of it. My brother is a fire whisperer, and we still have a fire extinguisher in every room of the house, despite the fact that he gained control years ago.

I've always been aware of my powers, so when I found out what they meant, it wasn't that big of a deal to me. Except for my name; I found my powers funny given that my name is Ivy. For the longest time, I didn't realize that not everyone could understand the plant life around them like it's an extension of their body—that awareness only came with our first lesson on whispering in first grade.

Everyone around me has always told me how lucky I am to be a plant whisperer, the rarest of the abilities, but I think they're just trying to make me feel better. It's not like I can contribute as much

as other whisperers. I've wondered if the reason that we're so rare is because of natural selection. Evolution favors traits that improve one's ability to survive, and us plant whisperers can't exactly fight off predators or people as well as others. The most we can do is figure out which plants are poisonous. Maybe we're becoming vestigial, like that useless arm tendon that some people don't have.

These thoughts were running through my head on my way to the mandatory, *Incredibly Important School Assembly*. Daisies growing around the base of a nearby tree called out to me for water in the soft, quiet tone characteristic of small flowers, so I made a quick diversion to water them. Afterward, I turned my thoughts back to the upcoming assembly. No one knew what it was about, not even the teachers.

As I sat down, I looked around for my brother, Owen, but I couldn't see him. He's a year younger than me and always determined to embarrass me at school by doing things like screaming my name or waving like a lunatic.

After everyone had settled into the auditorium, our principal Mrs. Sencter, walked out onto the stage with an uncharacteristically solemn expression on her face. "Ladies and gentlemen, as you may know, the world's governments have been trying to discover the most powerful whisperer alive for decades now."

I did not know this, and it seemed like not many others did either. How would they know that the person they discovered was actually the most powerful? What if someone more powerful was born at that moment? It didn't make much sense.

"Our government has narrowed their search down to one particular group of students at this school."

The room exploded with sound, with everyone was wondering what this meant. Some were excited, some were apprehensive, and others—like me—were curious about how the government was figuring this out, exactly.

"Calm down!" Mrs. Sencter yelled.

She continued to yell at the students until finally the vice-principal, Mr. Johnson, let out an ear-splitting whistle, shocking everyone into silence.

"Yes, thank you, Mr. Johnson," Mrs. Sencter said shakily. "The school has been informed that tonight, at 10 pm, the most promising candidates will receive an email containing all they need to know. Now, does anyone have any questions?" The room once again filled with deafening noise.

***

It was 9:50 on a Wednesday night, and I was procrastinating. My science homework was on the anatomy of plants, and, as boring as I thought my powers were, I still had an interest in plants and nature in general. Unfortunately, instead of motivating me to finish my homework, the interest had sent me down the deep dark hole of the Internet. I wasn't quite sure how I had ended up on a website called www.plantknowledge.com, and yet, here I was reading an article that I found fascinating.

Plant whispering has been researched the least out of all the powers—most likely because it is the rarest known power. However, research indicates there is more to it than it seems. Legends from many cultures, especially those in tropical regions, have mentioned

powerful whisperers that have been able to manipulate plants far beyond what modern societies have come to expect, and in some cases even communicate with them. This is different from the typical 'communication' that most plant whisperers experience, in which they instinctively know what a plant needs. Instead, plants have communicated fully formed ideas unrelated to their own survival, and, in one particular legend from India, been used to deliver a message to someone long after the original whisperer had died. Many scientists –

I was interrupted by a notification that pinged at the top of my laptop screen. My mind flashed to the assembly earlier that day. Was it possible? I clicked it, the anticipation building in my chest, but it wasn't what I was expecting.

Dear Owen Stear,

As you were told earlier today, the United States Government is searching for the most powerful whisperer in the country, regardless of whether they are an air, fire, water, plant, or earth whisperer. You are one of the potential candidates. Over the next few weeks, you will be subjected to challenges that will help us determine who the most powerful whisperer is. You will not be informed of what these challenges are, but know that we will be watching. One other person may know about your candidacy— only one. You may not tell anyone else, but your guardians have been informed. Please respond to this email with the name of your chosen person and their email.

Good luck,

The United States Government, Power Observation Division

Not only was the email rather creepy, but it wasn't even addressed to me. It was for my little brother.

"OWEN!" I yelled at the top of my lungs.

When he didn't respond, I walked over to my bedroom door and yelled again.

"IVY!" came his answering scream. "WHAT?"

Having gotten his attention, I walked to his room and shoved my laptop into his lap. I couldn't see his face while he read, but it was the picture of confusion by the time he got to the end of the email.

"What's this?" he asked. "What did you do?"

"Nothing," I responded, "it's probably a mistake. The difference in our school email addresses is one letter: ostear to istear. It's for you."

"I–I–." He stopped to clear his throat. "What does this mean?"

"Well, read what the email says. It tells you everything. Also, since I know that you're a *candidate*, you can't tell anyone else. Sorry."

I shrugged my shoulders and sighed. The words had come out harsher than I had meant them to, but in my defense, I hadn't quite figured out how I felt about it either.

The tightness in my chest reminded me of the time I lost the math contest to Jackie Michaels in 7th grade.

"So, then will you help me?" My confusion must have shown because he hurried on to clarify. "I mean, I don't know what the challenges are, but I should be prepared, right?"

I could see him starting to make mental lists.

"I should probably research what I can about all the known powers, especially fire whispering, see if anything like this has happened before…" His voice trailed off he continued to come up

with plans. Owen always tugged on his ear when he was nervous or worried, and right now it seemed like he was trying to tear it off.

Our parents had always emphasized that our jobs were to protect each other, and, no matter how annoyed at him I got, I never forgot it. I knew the same was true for him. "Okay," I agreed. "I'll help you."

***

It was only the day after I had agreed to help, and I was already regretting my decision. I was with my friend Jack in the library doing homework. Or at least, he was doing homework. About ten minutes back, I had once again fallen down the rabbit hole of the Internet. I skimmed many articles, but one, in particular, caught my attention:

Humans have lived with powers since we evolved into Homo-sapiens. We have yet to discover how we gained them, but the general consensus in the scientific community is that our brains respond to electrical signals all around us and react on a molecular level. With enough practice, one can gain a measure of control over these reactions, and when enough control is gained, the individual is considered to have 'mastered' their power. While most humans are born with some sort of power, be it earth, plant, fire, air, or water whispering, there are some who are born with the potential for a significantly greater amount of control than most people. These people are referred to as Mights and are few and far between, but are usually considered to be the most powerful whisperers in human history.

Huh. I wondered if that was what Owen was. I mean, it made sense for the most powerful whisperer in the United States to be a Might, but according to the article, it was rare.

How would we be able to tell? There was probably a test we could find somewhere. Once again, I felt my chest begin to tighten. *Why was Owen the powerful one? How—*

I squashed it down before it could get too far. Owen had asked for my help, and I was going to help him, no matter what. If only because he sucked at research and wouldn't stand a chance on his own. I was going to be a good sister.

I jolted out of my thoughts after Jack poked me especially hard in the shoulder.

"OW! What was that for?" I said, giving him a half-hearted angry expression.

"Finally," he responded. "I've been poking you for, like, a solid minute. What are you doing?" He leaned over to squint at my screen. "Um, I'm pretty sure that's not the homework."

I sighed. "Yeah, I know. I'm doing different research." I quickly emailed the website to myself and Owen, and then changed the subject. "So, anyway, how's your life?"

"Ivy."

"No, I'm serious, What's going on? I know that— "

"Ivy. Spill." Jack interrupted me again. He knew me too well for me to brush it off, and was looking at me with his stubborn *serious, must help my friends' look.* I sighed again and gave in.

"Fine. So—hypothetically—what would you do if your brother asked for help on something, and you want to help because he needs it, but you're also kind of jealous of him for it?"

Jack thought for a second before responding. "Okay, so your relationship with your brother is much better than mine, 'cause I probably wouldn't help him—not that he'd need my help in the first

place. You should probably still help Owen though. You love him, and all that."

"Wow, thanks Jack," I responded with a smile. "Super heartfelt."

He shrugged. "Yeah, well you know. I tried."

"I know. You helped–thanks. I'm going to help, but I'm still jealous. And then I feel terrible, because I think I should be happy for him, and I am, but I also just–ugh." I gave up on talking and just banged my head against the table in front of me, softly.

"I know you probably don't want to tell me," Jack chuckled. "But what exactly is this situation? You don't just seem jealous of him; you seem scared too."

"I guess, yeah. It'll be fine. Plus, I already told you, it's hypothetical," I mumbled.

I could tell that he didn't believe me, but thankfully, he didn't press the issue.

"Okay, Ivy. Maybe you should stop thinking about this 'totally hypothetical' situation, and just do your homework. The whole point of coming to the library was so you wouldn't get distracted."

At that, I finally picked my head up off the table and dug through my bag for a pencil. It was time to get to work.

***

A week later Owen and I were on our way to the school gym after having received emails about an opportunity for the candidates to practice their powers. Apparently, this *super secrecy* thing applied between candidates as well, so everyone had to go in at separate times. Owen's slot was at 5:30, and, for some reason, I was supposed to go with him.

The tightness in my chest was back during the walk, and I had to fight hard to ignore it. My job was to be a good sister, always. There was this time when I was six and he was five, that my mom had left me in charge of Owen for five minutes while she went to the bathroom. I got distracted by something at our restaurant table and didn't notice when he wandered off. I'll never forget the heart-stopping moment when I realized that he was gone, and the panicked few minutes that followed when I was sure that I would never see his chubby face again. Nothing was supposed to happen to him, and at that moment, I promised myself that nothing would. Unfortunately, at this moment my stupid feelings were interfering with my big-sister duties, and they had to stop.

As we walked into the gym, I gaped at the transformation. The usual basketball court was covered up by enormous blue mats, and all along the walls were great bowls of water, fire pits, plants, fans and boxes of soil. Standing in the middle of the room was Ms. Cervantes, the P.E. teacher, next to Mr. Rhodes, who taught the abilities class.

"Ah, Mr. Stear," Ms. Cervantes greeted Owen. She nodded at me. "Ms. Stear. As you can see, the gym has been transformed to fit any need that you may have. Mr. Stear, I know that you are a fire whisperer, so feel free to practice by the fire pits. Ms. Stear, you can help your brother, or practice your own powers, if you wish."

"Wait, really? That's it?" The words were out before I could stop myself. "Doesn't the government want us to do something? Why am I here?"

Mr. Rhodes spoke for the first time. "Yes, that's it, dear girl. This is a space for candidates to practice their abilities in preparation for the challenges to come." At my expression, he clarified hastily. "No, I

do not know what the challenges are. That is only for the government and Mrs. Sencter to know. As for you being invited, it was assumed that candidates would want their chosen person to help them. You are a fire whisperer, yes?"

"Um, no, I'm not." His look of surprise was expected. Usually, abilities ran in the family. Some were dominant over others, so it was pretty common for siblings to have the same power. "I'm a plant whisperer."

"A plant whisperer, really?" He looked at me with a renewed interest. "Curious. I've only had the fortune to teach a few plant whisperers in my career."

I nodded awkwardly and nudged Owen with my shoulder, not knowing what to do.

"Okay, thank you," he said to the teachers. "Should we go practice now?"

"Yes, of course. If you need anything, just ask. We're here to help," replied Ms. Cervantes.

As we walked towards the closest fire pit, I nudged Owen again. "That was weird."

"I know."

When we reached the fire pit, Owen immediately got to work. He lit fires, put them out, made shapes—whatever he could think of. Eventually, Mr. Rhodes came over and started giving him tips. That's when I wandered off to the closest planter box. To my horror, the flowers inside were practically crying out for water. So, I ran to the nearest bowl and brought some back for the plants.

As I poured it over the soil, I could have sworn that I saw a few new buds pop up, but I quickly dismissed it as a result of my imagination and poor observational skills. I couldn't help plants grow without extreme concentration, and it usually took a while.

"You know, there have been great plant whisperers who could manipulate plants at will."

I jumped. Mr. Rhodes was looking at the flowers over my shoulder, and I hadn't even heard him get close.

"They can make them immediately grow, shrink, contort, and even move without touching them."

"Wow." I didn't know what to say. "That's amazing."

"Yes, quite," he agreed. He then turned his attention to me, eyes big and owlish behind thick-rimmed glasses. "Can you?"

"What? No." I laughed. "Isn't that supposed to be a rare ability?"

"Huh. Okay." I could see the disappointment on his face. "So, how has it been, having a brother for a candidate?"

I blinked at the sudden subject change."It's been…okay. A bit weird. I feel like I've been helping him."

"Jealous at all?" he asked.

I thought about lying but decided against it. What was the point?

"A bit, I guess. I don't know," I said, shrugging.

My mind flashed back to my conversation with Jack.

"How would you feel if he was the most powerful whisperer?" Mr. Rhodes pressed.

"I don't know," I repeated.

That wasn't true. I would be incredibly jealous, even more so than now. Once again, I squashed down those feelings, taking a deep breath to loosen the tightness in my chest. It didn't matter how I felt because I had to support Owen.

Mr. Rhodes must have seen something in my face because he changed the subject back. "Okay then. Try."

"Try what?"

"Try to manipulate the flowers."

I looked over at Owen, who had his face screwed up in concentration. Was that the shape of a chicken in the fire in front of him? With Owen, you never knew. If he could manipulate his element, then maybe I could manipulate mine.

"Okay." I scrunched up my eyebrows in concentration, focusing solely on the plant, trying to get it to bend a bit to the right, but nothing happened.

I frowned and tried again, this time reaching forward to brush the leaves with my fingertips. All at once, I felt a rush of energy brush through my mind like a gentle breeze. When it was gone, there were eight words left in my mind: he speaks to wind and she to us.

I looked over at Mr. Rhodes, who was looking at me expectantly. The plant hadn't moved at all. Was it possible…? "

Are you an air whisperer?" I asked.

"As a matter of fact, yes, I am," he replied, looking a bit surprised. "How did you know?"

My mind started to spin with possibilities, none of them making the least bit of sense. "I don't know."

***

After that, Mr. Rhodes wandered back over to Owen, and I watched as they sparred, throwing fire and wind like weapons. Meanwhile, I tried over and over again to recreate that rush of energy, but nothing happened. There was the slightest inkling of something at the back of my mind, like I had learned about something like this in some class, but couldn't remember anything else. The memory was a delicate butterfly that fluttered further away the closer I got to it.

The butterfly disappeared completely once I noticed Ms. Cervantes waving us over to the center of the room. Our time was up.

"I've just been informed that the final ceremony will be in two days, on Saturday," she informed us.

I felt Owen starting to panic beside me, and his hand jumped up to pull on his ear. "Two days?"

"Yes," she said calmly. "You will receive an email with the exact details tonight."

My brother turned towards me, panicked. "Ivy, will you come with me?"

What else could I do? I squashed down the rising tide of jealousy and nodded.

***

The day of the final ceremony was a cold one, with dark clouds raining freezing cold water on us, and I wished that I was a water whisperer so I could stay dry without an umbrella. As we found our seats in the auditorium, I could feel Owen trembling next to me—not just from cold—and could see him physically restraining himself from tugging on his ear.

Suddenly, the lights turned off, rather ominously, and the room fell silent. Then, Mrs. Sencter walked onstage, accompanied by a rather scary-looking man in a crisp navy suit.

She picked up the microphone and began her speech.

"Welcome, candidates, friends, and family. This is Director Rory, head of the Power Observation Division of the United States Government. There have been a few changes to today's ceremony. First," she plastered a grand, fake smile on her face, "there will be no challenges. The most powerful whisperer has already been selected." Murmurs broke out amongst the crowd, and Owen turned to me, shocked. "The—"

Mrs. Sencter was cut off when Directed Rory leaned into the microphone, speaking for the first time. "The government has been observing the candidates, just as we said we would. The school has been a great help, and we've interviewed some of your teachers as well."

He had a deep, gravelly voice that sent shivers down my spine. "Certain circumstances caused us to expand our pool of candidates, and in it, we've discovered the most powerful whisperer that we have ever had the fortune to observe in the history of the department. The candidates were tested emotionally as well as ability-wise. Those of you who attended the optional training opportunity at school were observed, and those observations were invaluable in selecting the appropriate candidate. I would like to thank Ms. Cervantes for her help in testing our candidate. She has spent years mastering the art of plant whispering…"

Ms. Cervantes was a plant whisperer? I remembered the message that I had heard during the training session: He speaks to wind and she to us. Was Ms. Cervantes the *she* that it had been referring to?

"… She was able to leave a message for our whisperer, as a final test, and we're delighted to announce that our whisperer passed with flying colors…"

All at once, pieces began to snap together in my head, like a magnetic jigsaw puzzle. The messages… I had read about whisperers in India using plants to send messages. Was that what I had done? It was supposed to be extremely rare. Did Ms. Cervantes plant the message? And the 'circumstances' that Director Rory had referred to? Everyone knew that the government didn't like to admit their mistakes. What if the email they sent me…?

No. No, it couldn't be possible. I was just a boring girl with barely any powers. It couldn't be me. I felt my heart pounding in my chest, and my head began to spin. I had been told to go to Owen's gym session with him. Mr. Rhodes had asked me about my jealousy. Was that the final test? I sat, paralyzed with the fear of what I had just put together in my head, hoping beyond all hopes that it was just something that I had made up, that it wasn't true. As jealous as I had been of my brother, I had been scared for him too, because being the most powerful whisperer would be too much. No one wanted that kind of pressure from the government—or the world, for that matter. Especially not me.

I was so caught up in my own head that I missed Owen staring at me, fitting pieces together in his own head. I missed the volume in the room getting steadily louder, as soldiers dressed in black began to march down the aisles. I missed the soldiers stopping at my row as if awaiting further instruction. The only thing that snapped me out of it was the last sentence of Director Rory's speech, when he directed his unsettlingly pale grey eyes at me.

"I am pleased to announce that the most powerful whisperer in the United States of America is a Might named Ivy Stear."

That's when my old world crumbled around me—and my new one began.

The Form of a Poem

Bronté Bettencourt worked with Melody Xu to see that the form of her poem, *Yesterday Morning*, reflected her vision of the poem in the revision process.

Dear Reader,

Just as important as the words used for the content of the poem, is the form of the poem itself. The precision of Melody's words enables her to use the bare minimum on a vast page of white space, allowing her to capture the simplicity and tranquility of a moment of peace. Melody also leaves her sentences lowercase to convey the voice's smallness. With her attention for detail in mind, we went a step further by challenging the form of the poem itself.

First, Melody made certain that the word choice of her poem, *Yesterday Morning*, was exactly what she wanted. In this way, she ensured that she had a solid working structure. She removed extraneous words like "freezing," which she felt took away from the mood she wanted. She also added more content but just enough to keep the minimalist vibe going.

When Melody finalized the poem's content, she then messed with the form of the piece. In the first stanza she shifted the words "quiet and still," while also shrinking them sequentially. This added power to the words while adding to the quiet, serene tone of the piece. Melody experimented with the placement of the other stanzas, but ultimately chose to keep them in a traditional placement. What's important though is that Melody didn't choose their placements by default. After trial and error, she made an informed decision that stayed true to her vision of the poem.

My advice to you when writing poetry is to not accept the conventions of writing at face value. If you don't want punctuation, leave it out. If you want to write a standard rhyming poem then go for it. If you put a single word at the bottom of the page when all the content is up top, do it. But you should be aware of how your decisions impact the piece, be it traditional or experimental. Learn the rules, so that when you choose to break them, your writing has that much more meaning.

Happy Writing, and Break Wisely!

Bronté Bettencourt

Bronté Bettencourt graduated from the University of Central Florida with a bachelor's in Creative Writing. Recently, she earned her master's degree of Fine Arts in Writing for Children and Young Adult Literature from Hamline University. This is her second-year mentoring for the Society of Young Inklings Book Contest, which has proven as valuable as her college experience, as well as rewarding in helping aspiring authors. When she is not writing or working, Bronté is a full time D&D enthusiast, foodie, and YouTube connoisseur. Follow her on Medium, and Instagram @elliebronte.

Melody Xu

Melody Xu is a thirteen-year-old writer living in California with her family and dog. She's always liked writing, and *Yesterday Morning* is her first piece to ever be published. When not busy filling up note pads and book margins with poems, she enjoys reading and playing the flute.

Bronté Bettencourt : When did you start writing?

Melody Xu: I have always liked writing. When I was in elementary school I would type up a newsletter to my family, called *The Melody Times*. I wrote recaps of our family trips and interviewed my siblings. It was like a newsletter magazine. I sent it to all my family members every week and they really enjoyed it.

Q: Where did you draw inspiration from when writing this poem?

A: I don't really remember when I originally wrote it. I was flipping through my notebooks and I found a much shorter and more basic version of this poem, and I decided to start revising it. I think I might've been inspired by the first time I went rowing.

Q: What changed in your revisions for form?

A: Well, just like I do with all my poems, I started off really short, with a simple line, and then expanded it. I eventually added three more stanzas to this poem. My mentor inspired me to make format changes in the first stanza, rearranging the words a little bit to go along with the words.

Q: Where do you like to write?

A: Wherever I feel inspired that day. Usually at my desk, but sometimes I'll be going about my day and a line for a poem will pop up in my head. The other night I woke up at 3 AM with an idea for a poem, and I remember getting up in the dark just to jot it down.

Q: What advice do you have for other Young Inklings who don't like revising all that much?

A: I think you should always go into revising with an open mind. If someone ever gives you a suggestion and you don't seem fond of it right away, take it into consideration and try it out to see how you like it before making a final decision. You never know what you might like.

Yesterday Morning

by
Melody Xu

as the sun
peeks through the horizon
i am alone,

       quiet

          and

            still.

the water
wraps around me
on all sides
like a blanket
like i could fall asleep
in its arms.

i wonder
why every day
can't feel as peaceful
as this.

i engrave this memory
in my mind
before it inevitably evaporates
because nothing
this perfect
ever
lasts.

Scene Versus Summary

Devorah Berman worked with Julie Shi in revision on maintaining balance between scenes and summary to edit her story, *After the Storm*.

Dear Reader,

The first time I read, *After the Storm*, I was struck by how skillfully Julie wrote each scene, focusing on dialogue and action. She uses strong active verbs in her writing and develops her characters' personalities through the dialogue. There was very little summary at all. We decide to revise around this idea of scene versus summary.

First, we questioned which scenes were key to the plot. For example, the first draft started in the evening, and had Emma hear a strange sound, experience a thunderstorm, sleep and then get up. This lengthy opening took away from the tension of pursuing that "Hoo Hoo". Julie considered how to condense time. Instead of describing the storm in real time, she detailed the morning aftermath of a storm. By cutting that opening scene, Julie helped readers dive into the presenting problem.

Second, Julie looked at when summary is key to the plot. Emma tells the reader important information about her relationship with Mom in the breakfast scene. Emma pauses from the immediacy of the scene to summarize Mom's recent absence. Julie knew this summary moment was key to the later climax scene. So, she revised the ending to give a satisfying resolution to this moment of summary. She did this by calling back to Emma's earlier summary of Mom's absence. Then she enhanced the dialogue and action between Emma and Mom to create an authentic pay off.

As you edit your story, consider enhancing the scenes, as Julie did, with dialogue and action. Describe sensory details to put readers in the space. Then, go through your story again and consider the pace. Where does the detail get too dense? When would trimming benefit tension? Finally, think about your characters. Did you show their personalities and relationships in a scene or summarize them? If you told the reader about your character instead of showing, was that information important? Can you write a scene later in the story that shows the importance of that summarized detail?

Finding the balance between scene and summary is a useful editing tool!

Happy Writing,

Devorah Berman

Devorah Berman has a Masters in Fine Arts in Children's Writing from Hamline University. She loves sharing cool facts from her writing research (now including owl behavior thanks to Julie!) with her husband and three sons. She writes picture books and young middle grade. If a genie ever arrives at her doorstep, she will wish for the ability to draw.

Julie Shi

Julie Shi is a seventh grader who attends Harker Middle School in San Jose, California. She has loved reading ever since she was young and has developed her love of writing through those stories. She loves to dance and is on a dance team with many of her friends. Julie also enjoys drawing, math, and spending time with her family and friends. She loves nature and often finds ideas for her stories based on her natural surroundings.

Devorah Berman: Why do you enjoy writing?

Julie Shi: I like being able to create a new world, taking my cast of characters and making them do things in this new world. It's fun to come up with interesting plots and create personalities.

Q: How do you come up with your ideas?

A: Usually I base them off of real life. Or sometimes I have a strange dream and then I get an idea from that. But, usually it's from seeing things in everyday life. For this story, there was a really big storm one night. It was raining a lot. I was thinking it would be cool if there was something out there. I started imagining what it could be and thought up the owl. Then, when I started writing, I didn't plan everything. For example, with the owl attacks, I didn't plan for it to happen, but as I wrote the story I realized it needed to happen.

Q: What are your favorite books to read?

A: *A Series of Unfortunate Events.* I like reading *Nimona* and other graphic novels.

Q: Who do you enjoy sharing your stories with and why?

A: I like sharing them with my sister because she's a writer too, and she can look at my work from a different perspective. She's younger than me. We often share work with each other. Sometimes we just read each other's stories. Other times we help edit them.

Q: When did you start writing?

A: I don't really remember, probably around fourth grade. I guess I was reading books and decided it would be kind of cool if I had a story of my own.

Q: How did the process of revising feel for you?

A: I liked getting things from a different perspective. My mentor suggested edits made the story more realistic because she asked me to research what owls can and can't do. Some of the suggested edits didn't feel right. For example, I wrote a briefcase into a scene, even though it was hard. But, it didn't feel right, and I realized I could only make changes that felt true to the story.

Q: What is your writing process?

A: I usually write by myself. Sometimes I get good ideas and I write them down. I put all these pieces of paper with the ideas in my drawer. I come back to them later when I have time to write. Sometimes I forget about them. It's fun looking back at the ideas I came up with. Then I will take an idea and start working on a plot. I usually start with plot first and then develop the characters.

After the Storm

by

Julie Shi

Hoo, hoo…

I open my eyes to a melancholy sight. Golden autumn leaves, wet and torn from the storm, are scattered across the lawn and drifting in the pool. From my bed, I watch droplets of water trickle their way down the windowpane.

Hoo, hoo…

I turn my head to look at the clock on the wall. Seven o'clock in the morning. Groaning, I snuggle back into my blankets.

Hoo, hoo…

My mind finally registers the strange noise. What was that? I sit up and pause, hoping to hear it again.

Hoo, hoo…

By now, I am wide awake. Intrigued, I decide to investigate the noise after breakfast.

I head downstairs, my feet instinctively avoiding the creaking steps. As I enter the dark kitchen, I see a note on the refrigerator,

I'll be back late. Food in the fridge.

-Mom

I sigh, although I should be used to this already. Breakfasts are always like this these days. Mom seems never to have enough time anymore, not even enough to eat breakfast with me. Not hungry anymore, I decide, instead of eating breakfast, to solve the mystery of the noise. Grabbing my two-sizes-too-small-boots, I race outside in my T-shirt and sweatpants.

I am used to the cold, so waiting outside in my pajamas isn't a problem. For me, the air isn't cold—it is crisp and fresh and it smells like what it is supposed to smell like after a huge storm, like crushed pine needles and dewy grass. So I wait. I stand, silent, in my backyard, listening intently, hearing nothing but the sound of the distant wind. Then—

Hoo, hoo…

This time, it sounds pitiful, like a lost dog whimpering for its home. I try to pinpoint the location of the sound, but it's muffled, so I wait to hear it again so I can properly decide where it's coming from.

Hoo, hoo…

It seems to be coming from the bottom of a huge redwood tree, the tallest one in my backyard. I walk towards it, wondering what creature could be hiding in a tree and crying out so plaintively. As I near the tree, I heard it again, the ghost—

Hoo—

And then suddenly, a loud, clear, voice slices through the air, interrupting the moment and breaking the mysterious air.

"Who," the voice demands, "are you?"

I turn around and see a young boy, his red hair ruffled and

mud splattered all over his pants. A few inches shorter than me, he looks up at me like I am an enemy intruder in his palace. In his hands, he holds a basketball almost as big as he is.

"Who are you?" he asks again, his voice ringing through the backyard.

I stare at him. *This is my yard, not his, it strikes me. How can he just barge in and ask me who I am? He's trespassing in my property.*

"I am Emma," I say. "And this is my yard. What are you doing here? How did you get here?"

The boy frowns at me. "There was a hole in the fe–" He stops. "Wait," he whispers. "Do you hear that?"

All is silent again as we both pause, waiting. And then I hear it–a faint.

Hoo, hoo…

The boy gasps. "What was that?" he exclaims.

I glare at him, exasperated. *That is the sound I've been looking for!*

"Anyway, my name is Alex," the boy says. "And you can be my sidekick while I investigate that strange noise."

My mind is racing like a rocket, and I feel my anger begin to boil. *Help him investigate? I am the one who first found out about the noise!*

"Hey!" I say. "You can be my sidekick! And I don't even need your help." I pause. "But you can still be my sidekick."

"No," he says. "You are my sidekick, because I already know what is causing the noise."

"I do too," I say, even though I have no idea.

"Then tell me," Alex says.

"You tell me first," I reply.

"Fine! It's an owl, and it's in that tree over there," he proudly declares, pointing to the tallest redwood tree in my yard. "And the owl is probably hurt because of the storm last night. Bet you didn't think of that." He grins.

"That's what I was going to say," I pseudo-confidently retort, even though I am not sure what I was going to say. I suspected it was an owl, but an owl in my backyard?

We approach the tree together. The bottom is littered with wet leaves and bits of strewn grass. Dead bugs lie on the floor and torn branches are scattered everywhere. However, there is no owl.

"See?" I say. "I told you. No owl."

"But you agreed with me," Alex says, frowning at me.

Then we see a movement underneath a pile of leaves. The noise sounds again, much closer this time.

Hoo, hoo…

"It's under the leaves!" Alex exclaims, excited. He reaches towards the leaves and brushes them aside, revealing a tiny owl.

It is smaller than my hand and has huge yellow eyes and looks like a giant fluff ball. The owl lies on the ground, shivering. The moment it sees us, it hoo-es in fear, and attempts to scramble away.

"Don't worry," Alex coos. He reaches towards the owl. This only seems to scare the owl even more.

"Wait," I say. "You might get rabies."

"Owls don't carry rabies," Alex says.

"Yes they do," I insist.

"No, they do not," Alex responds.

I glare at him. He glares back at me.

"Either way," I say. "It might bite you."

Alex considers for a moment. "Well," he finally admits, "That's true. But then how do we help the owl?"

"Let's call the vet," I suggest. "If we try to help it ourselves, we might end up hurting it."

A raindrop falls onto my head.

"No!" Alex says. "This is our discovery! We have to save it!"

I frown, exasperated. "The vet can help the owl more than we can. Do you want to save it or not?"

Another raindrop falls onto my head. And another.

"But what if they mess up?" Alex questions.

"They're professionals," I say. "And we are children."

The raindrops fall down, softly at first. But soon, gaining speed, the raindrops pelt downwards onto the ground, soaking Alex, the owl, and me. Although we are under the redwood tree, the wind blows the rain towards us.

Great.

Hoo, hoo…

We both turn at the same time.

Hoo, hoo…

The owl hoo-es again, and desperately flaps its wet feathers.

"Oh no!" I cry. "The owl's getting wet! What do we do?"

Alex wipes raindrops out of his face. "Get a blanket!" he says. "Quick!"

"No!" I say. "A blanket will smoosh the baby owl! I'll get something else! Wait here," I say. I dash into my house, leaving a trail of muddy footprints everywhere, and grab a small plastic bag off of the kitchen counter.

At this moment, all that matters to me is saving the owl. I don't care if I get in trouble for leaving such a mess in the house. The only thing I can think about is the poor little owl in the rain, shivering with fright and from the cold.

Back in the heavy downpour, I see Alex squatting down in front of the owl, anxiously studying the owl's wet feathers. "Here!" I breathlessly gasp. I lay the plastic bag on top of the owl.

"I hope he's going to be all right," Alex murmurs.

"It could be a she," I instantly say.

"Well, I think it's a he," Alex retorts.

I open my mouth to say something, but then decide to let it go at that.

I squat down next to Alex and look at the owl. It is silent except for the splashing of the rain as Alex and I observe the little owl. It stays like that for a while. Alex and I squat in the pouring rain looking at the owl, which is now a bit used to us.

Suddenly, a huge shadow passes over my head. I look up and see a large owl with fierce yellow eyes and beautiful feathers silently descend down. It lands in front of the baby owl and me and flares its wings, its sharp glare penetrating me.

I can't help but notice how much larger it is than the baby owl. I also notice its razor-sharp beak and claws.

What if it hurts the baby owl? I panic.

The larger owl screeches and lunges towards us, extending his claws.

"No!" I yelp.

As the words leave my mouth, I realize what I have to do. I can't let all of Alex's and my hard work protecting the owl go to waste. Just as the larger owl is about to reach the smaller owl, I jump in between the baby owl and the larger owl, protecting the baby owl with my body.

The next moment is sudden confusion, a blur of feathers and shrieking. I feel sharp pains on my arms and see and feel nothing but the warm brown and grey of feathers. Just as quickly as it started, the chaos ends, and I find myself lying flat on my back, staring at the grey sky, gasping for breath. Something moves next to me, and I turn my head to see the baby owl. I instantly reach for it and grab it, cuddling it against my stomach.

"Yes!" I whisper, looking down at the baby owl. "You're safe!"

But then, suddenly, a sharp pain pierces my head. I cry out and look up in time to see the huge owl fly in for another attack. I curl up into a ball with the baby owl clutched to my stomach, praying for the larger owl to fly away. He doesn't. Instead, I feel another sharp twinge as the owl bites my hair, pulling and shrieking.

"Alex!" I cry, hoping that he is still here. "Get help!"

After a moment, Alex appears in the corner of my vision.

"Shoo!" he says, waving a stick at the large owl.

The owl shrieks and flutters in the air, almost knocking Alex off balance.

"I said get help!" I yell at him as the owl comes in for another attack, its claws scratching my bare arms.

Then I hear the backyard door slam open. "Let go of the baby owl!" a voice roars. "Roll away!"

The voice is very familiar, but I am in no state to try and remember who it belongs to. Instead, I comply, thumping the baby owl on the ground and roll away, my heart pounding in my chest.

Slowly, I sit up, in time for me to see the larger owl peck the baby owl.

"No!" I cry.

The larger owl shrieks at the baby owl. But then, the baby owl hoots happily, snuggling up to the larger owl. And the larger owl begins pecking at the baby owl. Not hurting it, I realize, but cleaning it.

Something clicks in my brain. The larger owl hadn't been attacking the smaller owl—it had been trying to rescue it. The mother owl had come back for its baby after all. While watching the lonely baby owl, I had just assumed that its mother had abandoned it.

"Are you okay?" the voice cries behind me.

The same voice that told me to let the owl go. I turn around, and my eyes open in surprise.

It's Mom.

Mom, who doesn't have time for breakfast anymore, who is too busy with work, is here, in my backyard?

"Emma!" Mom cries. "Are you okay?"

Speechless, I just nod. Mom wraps me in a hug, almost lifting me up. Then she bustles me into the house, saying something about bandaging me up. Mom tuts softly as she sees my muddy tracks.

Suddenly, I start to cry. Maybe it's the cuts the mother owl gave me, maybe I'm just relieved that I survived the incident, or maybe it's my mind being overwhelmed by what has happened today, but I am now bawling, tears sliding down my cheeks as I try to wipe them away.

Mom rushes over and envelopes me in a hug again, patting me soothingly and repeating the words, "It will be okay, Emma. Don't worry. Everything will be fine."

Finally, I find my voice. "Why did you come home early?" I ask. "Aren't you busy?"

There is a pause, and then Mom answers.

"Oh," she says. "Just a feeling. I wanted to come home to surprise you, and I guess I got lucky."

The next morning, after breakfast, I walk to Alex's house and ring his doorbell. It's Alex that answers the door. He doesn't look very surprised to see me.

"The owls will have to stay in my backyard for a while," I tell him.

Alex's eyes widen. "The owls are still in your yard?" he asks.

"Yeah," I respond. "They will be able to leave when the baby owl learns how to fly. But we can't go into my yard until they leave."

Alex looks at me enviously. "Lucky!" he says. "You have a real live owl in your backyard!"

"Two real live owls," I correct him.

"Two real live owls!" he grins.

I nod. Then I notice that Alex is holding a basketball in his hands.

"Want to play?" I ask him.

"Sure!"

Secondary Characters

Kalena Miller aided Maizie Ferguson in a big revision challenge - developing secondary characters to add complexity and depth to her story, *Bluegrass*.

Dear Reader,

Developing complex, interesting, and believable characters is a difficult task for any writer. When writing a story with a diverse cast of characters, that challenge becomes even more daunting.

When I first read Maizie's story, *Bluegrass*, I was impressed by the thought she had put into crafting her main character. Dixie, the protagonist, is both compassionate and fearful, friendly, and shy. Thanks to Maizie's skillful character development, readers can easily relate to Dixie's insecurities and struggles with anxiety. However, there were secondary characters in Maizie's story that were less developed. While it's normal for secondary characters to be less detailed than the protagonist, I knew Maizie was a strong writer, and I challenged her to add complexity to her story.

We talked about two strategies for developing secondary characters. The first is to write a descriptive paragraph when a secondary character is first introduced or during an important scene involving that character. This allows the writer to focus on the key aspects of the character and immediately shape the reader's perception. For example, in Bluegrass, Maizie includes concise, beautifully-written descriptions of Mom and Dad that show the reader how these characters have shaped Dixie's life.

The second option is revealing details about secondary characters gradually through physical description, dialogue, and action. Maizie employs this technique with Lizzi-Jo, Dixie's best friend. We first learn that Lizzi-Jo is kind and helpful. Then, we find out that Lizzi-Jo is a perfectionist who can be selfish. At the end of the story, Maizie shows Lizzi-Jo to be a flawed but understanding friend.

I encourage you to try both of these techniques when crafting characters in your own writing. As you'll see in *Bluegrass*, compelling secondary characters add depth to your writing and keep readers engaged in your story.

Happy Writing,

Kalena Miller

Kalena Miller received her BA from Carleton College and her MFA from Hamline University. She currently lives in Hopkins, MN where she writes fiction, runs an editorial business, and teaches creative writing classes for children. When she's not writing (or talking about how she should be writing), Kalena enjoys cooking, scrapbooking, and convincing her dog that squirrels are not invading their home.

Maizie Ferguson

Maizie is a musical seventh grader who lives in Olathe, Kansas and is homeschooled. She loves nostalgic old movies, curling up with a good book on a rainy day (and on sunny days, too), acting out her favorite book scenes with her sister, and watching for story ideas everywhere she goes. She has been writing short stories since she was eleven.

Kalena Miller: What inspired you to write *Bluegrass*?

Maizie Ferguson: I thought about the place, Bluegrass, Kentucky. I also like to think of cool names–like Dixie, the main character. It really came together after that. I liked the challenge of writing a short story, of making these characters real, and saying everything I wanted to say in that short space.

Q: How did revising your secondary characters change your story?

A: I think it added depth. You understood the characters more because of their backstory. I think it made the characters make more sense and it made them more real.

Q: Was it difficult to write about a character younger than you?

A: No. That's why I really liked this story because I was going back into my memory of when I was that age and stories I've read about characters that age. I really like how it turned out because I feel like the main character is very believable for her age.

Q: Where do you like to write?

A: Well, I usually write on the computer. And it's by a lot of the windows in our dining room. The windows show into our backyard and it opens into a green space.

Q: Do you like to read? If so, what are your favorite books?

A: I love to read. I love the *Penderwicks* series by Jeanne Birdsall. I like a lot of Rick Riordan's books. I like *To Night Owl From Dogfish* by Holly Goldberg Sloan and Meg Wolitzer. I love a lot of different things. I have a ton of favorite books.

Q: What advice would you give to other young writers?

A: To not stop writing even when your story isn't turning out the way you want or you have writer's block. You have to keep writing. Inspiration is everywhere. You can observe things through the perspective of a writer.

Bluegrass

by

Maizie Ferguson

August is the worst month.

I can think of about a million reasons why, but I'll tell you three:

School starts.

The public library closes until September because of new book shipments.

It's the month—last year—when my mom left my dad and me.

But that is not the worst part.

I have a terrible fear of public speaking.

I am very shy, which is why I am afraid.

I am afraid because every August, they hold the Bluegrass, Bluegrass Festival.

Every August, before the Bluegrass, Bluegrass Festival, there is a speech.

Every August, for the speech, they pick a speaker from the fifth grade.

I am in the fifth grade.

And they picked me: Dixie Matthews.

***

It happened in the library. It was Saturday, and I was there because the library closes for the month in August, and when that happens, you get to keep the books you check out for the whole month. I used to not like the library because I've always had trouble reading. I've been below my grade level for a long time, but a couple of months ago everything clicked! I like reading now, although I'm still not up to grade level… yet.

Anyway, I was reading aloud to myself from *Clementine*, my favorite book in the universe, when Mrs. Grimes, the head librarian who sneaks up on readers, tapped my shoulder. I swallowed.

"Hi Trixie." She waggled her fingers at me.

I clenched my teeth. She always gets my name wrong!

"It just so happened that I should hear your nice voice. What are you reading?"

I showed her the cover of my book.

"Ah, such a funny story! Say, what grade are you going into, Bixie?" I closed my eyes and held up five fingers.

"Brilliant!" she smiled. "Now, how would you like to give a speech?"

I swallowed again. *A speech? Oh no! It couldn't be, the speech, could it? But I am going to be in the fifth grade…oh no. How was I supposed to give a speech when I couldn't even talk to a librarian?*

"Uh…hmm…I…uh…" I managed.

"Double brilliant!" She shook my hand. "Talk about what

Bluegrass is to Bluegrass, Kentucky. To you. Thanks so much."

I felt shaky as she walked away. My fingers trembled. I bit my lip to keep from crying.

She turned around, "And don't forget that the festival is always on the second Saturday in August…so make sure your speech is done in one week! Thank you again, Chrissy!" she waved.

I didn't wave back. I thought about how I was going to look like a complete fool in front of the whole entire city of Bluegrass, Kentucky. Maybe even the whole Turnpike Valley!

I checked out my books, and tried to smile. But I knew even happy Clementine couldn't make me feel any better.

***

I blink in the hot sunlight. White spots dance before my eyes, and I heft a sack of ripe tomatoes to my left arm. My hair feels hot and sticky to the back of my neck. Only two more houses to go until Aunt Cass's. The heavy tomatoes bump against my side. But I don't pay attention; I can't stop thinking of the speech.

Today is Sunday, Mr. Thornwood's sharing day. He always invites me over to get some fresh vegetables from his garden to take back to Aunt Cass. Mr. Thornwood is a retired literature professor. He says his second home used to be the library, but he doesn't get out much anymore. In exchange for his garden's crop of the week, I bring him his requested reading. As I give him his books, he peeks into my bag, sees mine and gives me an approving nod. He knows how hard I've been working.

Sunday also means there are only six days until the festival.

And I haven't even told Aunt Cass. The speech hangs over me like a storm cloud. A hot one that refuses to rain. I drag my feet, then remember that I am calling Dad at 4:00 p.m. I rush into the kitchen.

3:57. I drop the tomatoes on the counter and see that Aunt Cass is baking something. A waft of spice-filled air wraps me in a cinnamon hug. I take a deep breath, feel my racing heart slow down, and log onto her laptop.

Dad is in Dubai where it's midnight. That makes for a late night for him, but he says I'm worth it. We talk and I forget all about the speech. For a while everything is all right.

An hour later, I tell him good night and set the table for dinner. Aunt Cass makes a salad with Mr. Thornwood's tomatoes, sprinkling them with salt, pepper and dill. I grab a whole tomato and bite a chunk out of it. I still don't tell her.

I feel almost ready to tell her after dinner but then she starts reading her mystery novel for book club. She has left it for last minute like always, and I know it's not a good time.

I go upstairs to my room, scrawl a quick note on the back of a note card, and drop it in the basket right outside my window. I pull on the ropes, and the pulley pushes the basket to the window right across from mine.

Almost immediately, the window opens and Lizzi-Jo McKinnon takes my note, flashing me a braced smile. I don't wait for an answer. I run and slide down the banister to the back door. There's a knock.

Without looking up from her book, Aunt Cass calls. "Dixie, won't you get that?"

And I do. It's Lizzi-Jo. She takes my hand.

"Ready?" she asks.

Before I can answer, Aunt Cass peers at us over her novel, "Hi Lizzi-Jo! My mini bundt cakes should be cool enough for you two to try. You've eaten dinner? I don't want to spoil it if you haven't."

She nods vigorously, "Yes."

Aunt Cass smiles, then adds. "You seem to have a knack to know when my oven timer goes off."

As she cuts slices of the cinnamon goodness, Aunt Cass winks at Lizzi. Aunt Cass has a baking business and Lizzi and I have become her unofficial taste testers. Think of the best cake you've ever had. These little treats were ten times better.

After we're done, we run up to my room and jump on my beanbag chair. Lizzi-Jo is my best friend. She will be in the fifth grade, like me, but has been reading way above our grade level for a long time. She's in the gifted program at our school, and is also my summer reading tutor.

"What book today?" I ask her.

Lizzi reaches into my library bag and pulls out a book: *Judy Moody and the Bucket List*.

"This is one of my favorites. That's why I had you check it out. It's funny like *Clementine*. And Judy Moody is a third grader, too!"

I grin and open it up. "Sunflower seeds, Sharpie, super glue. She, Judy Moody was pawing through Grandma Lou's purse..."

***

The next morning, I decide I am ready to tell someone about the speech. Lizzi-Jo is the first name that pops into my head. And I know exactly where to find her: next door. I wait until after lunch, and I go up to the front porch, and knock.

Mikey McKinnon opens the door. He is Lizzi's 14-year-old brother.

"Hey Strawberry!" he says to me.

He calls me strawberry because I have red hair. I kind of freeze. It's hard for me to talk to people other than Dad, Aunt Cass and Lizzi. I struggle to figure out what to do.

"Do you want Liz?" he asks me.

I nod.

He smiles, "Okey-doke! She's up in her room."

"Thanks," I whisper.

I rush past him, and I'm up the stairs in a flash. He's right. She is in her room playing cello while reciting equivalent fractions and reading *Pride and Prejudice* (which she's read three times before because loves Jane Austen). Did I tell you she was great at multitasking, too?

She sees me, "Dixie! Awesome! Just let me finish this song."

Once finished, she puts the book on her bed, and packs up her cello.

"That was great!" I tell her. "And I have something to tell you. It's really important."

"Okay..." She smiles at me, curious.

"I was picked to give the speech for the Bluegrass, Bluegrass Festival on Saturday and I need help."

Her face falls. She looks confused.

"What is it?" I ask her.

She starts to pace. "How did I forget? It's always the second Saturday of August. Fifth grade! I should've known!" Her voice rises and she slaps her forehead with her palm.

Then, she starts yelling in a foreign language I do not know, and seeing that I am invisible to her, I run down the stairs, tears streaming down my face.

Mrs. McKinnon doesn't notice me and starts up the stairs.

Mikey does, "Hey, Dixie, wait!"

But I am already out the door. Now, I really have to tell Aunt Cass. At home, I run in and hug Aunt Cass. The tears just flow.

"Oh, sweetie!" she exclaims. "What's wrong?"

I can't talk, so she just holds me until I can. We sit there for a long time, silent. And then, I tell her the whole entire story.

"Why did she have to pick me? She knows I'm terrible at reading and it'll be awful!" I wail. "She doesn't even know my name!"

Aunt Cass pulls me out at arm's length, "Dixie, you should've told me sooner. Darling, you are not terrible at reading, for one thing. And well, I've known Mrs. Grimes since we were girls. She's never been able to remember anyone's name! But she's always seemed to know what was best for people. I just think that Mrs. Grimes knows how hard you are working on reading, and maybe wanted to give you an opportunity to show off your skills."

When I don't say anything, Aunt Cass shakes her head smiling. "You should've heard how she butchered the name Cassandra. It's been much easier for her since I started going by Cass."

I laugh. Aunt Cass always can make me laugh. We sit there, together and I just want to stay like that forever. She tells me she'll try to set aside some time for me, but just not now. Her church group is meeting soon to feed the homeless. Help will have to wait until she's not so busy.

Mikey McKinnon comes over to "keep me company." I don't need someone to watch me, but he is next door and I know Cass thinks someone should be over here because she can't be with me. Mikey plays in a bluegrass band at the high school. He's lugged his

bass over to use this time for practice. I am sitting on the couch and he sits down next to me.

"Hey," he says. "You probably don't want to talk about earlier, but we can."

I shake my head no, but he continues.

"This will all blow over soon. Give her a couple of days and she'll cool off. Liz can be intense sometimes—she's such a firstborn. It's like we were born out of order. You know… she's a high achiever and a big perfectionist, but she's also not so good with surprises. Me, I'm more laid back. I get good grades and all, but I'd rather be playing my music." He pats my shoulder and stands up. I'm still quiet. And he doesn't seem to mind.

That's one of the things I love about Mikey. He's so understanding. I am tired, so I go upstairs and flop onto my bed. I leave my door open so I can listen. The slow, low melodic notes help me forget about the speech and even Lizzi as I drift off into dreamland.

***

I cannot believe I only have four days left until the speech!

I'm lying on the floor of my bedroom, the back of my neck pressed on the cold wood planks, trying to think of words. Any words. Anything. "Bluegrass is part of our blood… basses and banjos… songs together in the summer…" It doesn't seem right. And the 'not right' feeling reminds me of Mom.

My mom was a good mom… until she wasn't. She left us a year and three days ago and it wasn't until she left that dad found that we were in monstrous debt. Debt, because Mom had a gambling problem—a big gambling problem. She lost all of our money. After that, Dad became worried about everything. Until the phone call.

My dad is an engineer. I don't exactly know what that is, but when he has to travel, he's usually consulting on projects and he's only gone for a few days. This new project was different. He would manage the whole thing and it would be overseas. In Dubai.

I was shocked that Dad would say yes to this because we are really close. I have needed him more since Mom left. He told me that he had requested this job. He said that this could be the job that could get us up and out of debt. And he said I couldn't go with him.

He didn't know what Dubai would be like for a ten-year-old girl. He wanted to protect me. He also didn't know how long it would take. At least six months, maybe a year or a year and a half. He just didn't know. Aunt Cass is his sister and our only relative. So here I am.

It's 4:00 p.m. and I feel ready to tell Dad about the speech. I don't want to worry him, but I feel like it's the right thing to do. But when he starts talking about his job and I tell him about how weird Lizzi-Jo is acting and that she's not talking to me, it gets too late.

***

Three! That's the number of days left until the festival.

Aunt Cass and I do research on Bluegrass for my speech, and I practice my reading alone. Since Lizzie-Jo seems to be avoiding me, I try to think of every way possible to communicate with her. I send her mail in our pulley, I give letters to Mikey, I put a sign in my window, and I throw paper airplane messages in through the mail slot. Nothing works. I don't get anything in return.

***

Two more days till the speech.

Aunt Cass tells me to go weed the back flower beds. She wants me to take my mind off of the speech by doing normal things.

"Here comes the sun little darlin'. Here comes the sun and I say, It's all right…" I sing as I weed.

The hot sun is blaring down on my head, making my scalp feel itchy.

Aunt Cass appears in the doorway. "Come inside and wash your hands!" she commands.

Am I in trouble? It sure sounds like it.

I put down my trowel and follow her. I blink. My eyes are still getting used to the indoor light. She's sitting in the kitchen. She folds her hands and leans forward on the table.

"Dixie Webster Matthews," she says. "Sit down."

I sit down and she opens up her palm. She offers me a piece of chocolate. *What?*

"Chocolate makes you think better. True fact." She smiles at me. "I want you to work on your speech now without any distractions. I'll let you use the laptop while I go to the grocery store. I'm about out of flour! Be a good girl, sweetie." She smiles again, and I know I was never in trouble.

"I love you. And thanks for the chocolate," I tell her, popping it into my mouth.

She leaves and the click of the door makes me jump. I open the laptop and stare at the angry cursor blinking on the blank white page. I take a deep breath, think of Dad, and I write.

***

It's Friday. The speech is tomorrow.

I haven't talked to Lizzi-Jo for four whole days. My heart hurts so much. I want to shout out–*Hey, remember me*–when I see her getting the mail or hula-hooping in her driveway. But I don't say a word. Aunt Cass wants me to read my speech to her. But I just can't and I feel like a failure.

If I can't read the speech to my aunt, I won't be able to read it to hundreds, maybe thousands of people!

When I call Dad, I mostly listen to his stories of the project. I don't think I say anything other than "hi" and "I love you." I don't eat dinner. I can't make one single macaroni go down my throat. Aunt Cass offers me a cupcake but I can't eat that either. I cry myself to sleep with the quiet lull of the breeze and the soft snoring of Aunt Cass in the next room.

***

Today is the speech!

I wake up, and the horror of people and disaster crowds my brain. Aunt Cass makes cinnamon toast, my favorite, but I can barely manage a bite.

The festival starts at 11:00 a.m. with me reading my speech. Then, there is a big banquet and Bluegrass music contests, concerts, lessons, and a whole fair, too! Last year, we didn't go.

Too many people make me feel overwhelmed. And this year,

I'm only reading the speech. Then, I'm going home.

It's 10:00. Aunt Cass puts my hair into two French braids. She says it's a flattering style for someone with red hair. I guess. I am too anxious to pay much attention to her.

I put on a purple sundress and sandals. Aunt Cass twirls me around in front of the hall mirror. I have to admit, I look good. I read my speech in the bathroom one last time.

"Ready to go, Dixie?" Aunt Cass hollers up the stairs.

"Almost," I call as I rush into my room, grabbing the two friendship bracelets I made yesterday.

They match. I tie one on my wrist, knowing exactly what I'm going to do with the other.

The Bluegrass, Bluegrass Festival is located in a big field which holds the county fair in June and the carnival each fall. The crowds are already thronging toward the stage. Surrounding everyone, everywhere, are big white tents. The Ferris wheel is spinning in anticipation.

I leave Aunt Cass with one of her book club friends and climb a tree to see better. I can't see anyone I know, except Aunt Cass. Then, I realize I am doing this all wrong. I need to go where I know she will be, her favorite place during carnivals and county fairs. I climb back down and run through the crowd, not stopping even when I bump into people. I clutch the bracelet and stop at the cotton candy cart, panting as she turns around.

"Goodness, Dixie, are you okay?" Lizzi-Jo looks worried.

"No," I tell her simply. "And, I don't know if you want to be my friend anymore, but I want to give you this." I thrust out the bracelet.

She cups it in her hands and blows out air. "You know, I'm sorry about how terrible I acted on Monday. I… I was jealous because I'm ahead in reading and everything, and well, I thought I deserved it." She hangs her head and continues. "My brother was the reader when he was in fifth grade. I guess I felt like I should do it instead of you. And I feel really bad knowing I could've helped you. It was so hard not talking to you. I have a whole basket of your notes. And you know what? I'm going to answer every. Single. One."

I laugh, then hug her, hearing her voice quiver.

"I'm never going to do anything like that again." She half grins. "Those were the hardest four days ever!" I tie the bracelet on her wrist and we join hands.

Just then, the mayor of Bluegrass, Kentucky finds me and leads me onto the stage. People are everywhere as far as I can see. The sun is hot. After everyone claps for me, the air goes dead silent. Silent, except for the cicadas.

I adjust the microphone. I take a deep breath and speak into it, but that horrible static sound happens. A few people cough. A few people laugh, and I wish I could sink down into the earth and disappear. I look out again, and see people impatiently looking at their watches and shading their eyes. Then, something yellow moves upward. It's Lizzi-Jo! In a tree. She waves crazily to get my attention, her yellow dress making her look like a perched canary. She points to her bracelet and nods at me encouragingly.

I take another deep breath and think of everyone this speech is for… Aunt Cass, Dad, Lizzi-Jo, Mikey, Mr. Thornwood, even Librarian Grimes. It's for everyone. And I begin.

"Bluegrass music is a type of music that was born in the Bluegrass state, here, Kentucky. It's a combined mixture of Scottish and

Irish immigrant songs as well as Appalachian music, African-American spirituals and the blues. It is played on many instruments, the most well-known being the banjo, the fiddle and the bass.

"Why is this town called Bluegrass, Kentucky? Because bluegrass is in our blood! In each and every one of us. You may know someone who plays bluegrass. I have a good friend, Mikey McKinnon, who plays bluegrass on the bass. And I think that even if you don't play it, it's still part of your blood. Because you live here. Bluegrass, Kentucky isn't just about bluegrass music, it's about family and friends.

My Aunt Cass took me in last year when my dad needed her to and I think that even if you weren't born here, you can still have bluegrass blood. Everyone here helps each other, and everyone makes everyone feel part of the community.

I know everybody doesn't get along all the time. I recently learned that with my best friend, Lizzi-Jo. You may be friends for months, and then not for a week, and then maybe you'll be friends forever. Bluegrass for us isn't just music or our town. It's us. We are bluegrass. Our community is bluegrass. And bluegrass, of course, is in our blood. Thank you."

I close my eyes for a moment, listening to the silence. Then, a thunderous noise is everywhere. I open my eyes. People are clapping! They are clapping for me! Whistling and shouting and clapping and stomping. It feels wonderful to be up on a stage, knowing that everyone is clapping for me.

The mayor comes up and speaks into the microphone, "Thank you so much, Dixie, that was one of the best speeches I've ever heard."

He is looking straight at me, and I think I see tears in his eyes.

"And now, let the Bluegrass, Bluegrass Festival begin!" he

yells. The mob of people expands and rushes in different directions. I walk down the steps to find Aunt Cass and Lizzi-Jo.

"I'm so sorry ma'am!" I whisper when I bump into a lady standing in front of me.

She turns around. It's the librarian, Mrs. Grimes! I hold my breath.

"That was amazing," she tells me, dabbing her eyes.

"Thank you," I reply. "And Mrs. Grimes?"

"Yes, dearie?" She smiles wide.

I take a deep breath, "After you picked me, I was really wondering why. But Aunt Cass told me that you've always had a knack for knowing what people need and when. I realize now that I needed that speech."

We both turn to walk away, but then she speaks again, "I'm so glad I was right about you. Well done, Dixie."

I find Lizzi again, by the cotton candy stand. "Great job!" she tells me.

I hug her and say, "Thanks! I'm going to go. You know me and big crowds."

"Okay. Reading lesson tomorrow?" she asks.

"You betcha!" We high five.

I go off to find Aunt Cass. She's by the same tree I had climbed earlier.

"Sweetie, that was wonderful! You truly were amazing. I told your dad about the speech on Monday, the same day you told me. I hope it's all right…"

"Oh yes, Aunt Cass!" I hug her.

"And he asked me to FaceTime him so he could see it live,"

she continues. "He loved it and wants you to call him when we get home, okay?"

I smile. "Thank you!"

When we get to our driveway, Aunt Cass dials the number. I sit on the front steps, her phone to my ear.

"Daddy?"

"Hi sweet Dixie, you were amazing!" he tells me.

"I was pretty nervous," I admit.

"Well, I'm so proud of you conquering your fear."

"Thanks! Aunt Cass helped."

"What about Lizzi-Jo, hon?" he asks me.

"We're all good now. I love you, Dad!"

"I love you so much, too. I wish I could hug you right now." He sounds so happy.

"Me too!"

And then, I see him. He walks around the side of the house, his phone to his ear.

"Dad? Dad!" I scream, running towards him.

He scoops me up in his arms.

"My Dixie," he whispers in my ear.

Dixie and Dad, together at last.

In Bluegrass.

Dialogue

Philomena Block worked with Austin Moon to revise dialogue in his thrilling story, *Hephaestus Falls*, a telling of Greek mythology.

Dear Reader,

Stories allow the characters in our heads to come to life. This is made even more real by the way our characters communicate with each other. When I met with Austin to revise his story *Hephaestus Falls*, we decided to play with dialogue to see how that would add to his very exciting story of Greek mythology.

Austin's characters are all from Greek mythology, so the first step he took was discovering what made his version of the characters who they are. As an exercise, Austin drew a few of the key characters in his story to help him flesh out the details of their appearances. For example, we found out that Austin's version of Hephaestus has a large mohawk and blue overalls. These details helped dictate how his version of Hephaestus is different from a classic toga-clad Greek god and informs the reader how the character speaks. Austin is fascinated with comic books and this was a very useful and fun activity for developing his characters.

In his revision, Austin focused on two main parts of the dialogue—inner monologue and talking between characters. Hephaestus has amnesia in the story, but even though he doesn't know who he is, he still is able to react to the situations around him. We used inner monologue and reactions to help show the reader more about a character who doesn't know much about himself.

From his reactions, we can tell he is young, strong, and has a good sense of humor. We also looked at the description and differences in speaking between characters. We played with varying the description and limiting using he/she "said" after dialogue. The more specific the language around the dialogue the more realistic and intriguing the dialogue itself becomes. Austin used character specificity to make the way the characters speak different from each other and more distinct. He made Atlas speak much more casually and simply to work as contrast to his brother, Prometheus. He also chose to have Zeus speak in ALL CAPS to show the power and force in his voice.

If you are writing a story based on mythology or other established characters, you might want to try Austin's approach. Grab some paper and draw what the characters look like in your head. Use your pictures to imagine how they might speak, and insert that specificity to your story.

Cheers!
Philomena Block

Philomena Block is an actor, writer, and comedian originally from Santa Cruz, California. Philomena holds two bachelor's degrees—one in musical theatre, the other in psychology—and is trained in playwriting, sketch comedy, and improvisation. Philomena has always been drawn to storytelling and loves developing characters onstage and on the page. Philomena worked as a teacher with Society of Young Inklings for two years and is so happy to keep supporting young writers with the Inklings Book Contest. When Philomena isn't writing or performing, she works as a marketing professional and loves breathing in the ocean air.

Austin Moon

Austin Moon is in fourth grade. He lives in Minneapolis, Minnesota. In his spare time, he likes to make short films, read, and write. He loves comics and hopes to someday be a comic writer in Denmark. His favorite animal is the peregrine falcon because it is super-duper fast.

Philomena Block: Why do you like writing?
Austin Moon: I like writing because it is a way to compile anything on paper (or Google doc) and use my thoughts to turn them into stories.

Q: Where do you usually write and what do you usually write with?
A: I usually write in the morning and on my laptop because when I wrote a book of short stories, I got used to that way of writing. I like to write this way because it makes it easier to do revisions.

Q: What changed when you revised your story?
A: The characters' way of talking changed. I added Greek words. The character, Atlas, changed and now speaks more… simply. Another thing that changed was the description changed a bit. Hephaestus's thoughts were a big change. And the way Hera reacts in the end changed a lot.

Q: How did you feel revising your story?

A: I felt proud. My story is as close to being the best it can be. It was a little frustrating because it was my first time revising something, and it felt a little hard finding the opportunities to change things.

Q: How do you feel about your story now?

A: I feel it is more ready for readers than before the series of revision. I feel much better about my story now.

Q: Anything else you want to share with young writers?

A: Reading (and video games sometimes) are great ways to find inspiration for writing.

Hephaestus Falls

by
Austin Moon

Author's Note: I used some Greek words in this story. Geia sas is hello, fotia is fire, mellontikos is future, antio sas is goodbye, oikogeneia is family.

I was falling. I didn't know anything except that my name was Hephaestus. Where I was falling from, I did not know. I had no idea who my father was, or my mother. I was in deep pain. My eyes stung as the wind beat against my face. I felt like a newborn wood duck, just moving from my nest.

For some sad, sad, reason, I had a large mohawk. I was wearing a cheesy wool sweater (I was way too hot) under a pair of buttoned blue overalls. Also, I was wearing boots that looked like something from the first draft of a superhero costume. Ugh.

I pinched myself. I had to know if I was dreaming. Nothing happened. I just kept falling.

My blood had rushed to my head. It felt horrible. The pressure of the strong wind against my body hurt tremendously. My legs felt incredibly light, which stung.

Where was I? Who were my siblings? Did I have siblings?

I tried to answer these questions. But nothing came up. I looked down. I could not yet see a shape, nor a person. I felt like an unsuspecting deer who had fallen prey to a hunter's trap.

Then suddenly, I moved. I must've been several hundred feet high, because the tiny world below me made me feel like a giant. I could see several clouds around me.

Then, I looked down. I saw my feet. My left foot was deeply swollen. It must be the main source of my pain. The longer my foot was left unattended, the more it hurt. I screamed.

Someone must have heard me, for a few seconds later a figure came into view. I could not comprehend who it was, for I seemed to not be able to see clearly. It came closer into view. The figure was tall. It seemed to be running away from something. No, someone. The figure looked like a man, only taller. Much taller. His size was titanic. He was wearing shorts, sandals, and a belt. He had a wristband on his right arm. Also, his hair curved upward on the left and right sides of his head.

"Who are you?" I asked.

The figure only stared at me, as if it was a miracle that I could talk.

"I said, who are you?"

The figure stopped staring at me, and spoke.

"I am the Titan Prometheus. Geia sas. And you are?" Prometheus snapped.

I was baffled to realize that I knew the Greek language.

"Hephaestus," I said.

A look of terror appeared on the Titan's face. He paused. I looked at his right hand. He held a torch, only instead of wood, he had a plant of some sort.

"Why are you holding fire?" I asked, inquisitively.

Prometheus still looked puzzled. "Why should I tell you that? I just met you!" he bellowed.

I started to lose my patience.

Prometheus finally decided to speak. "I stole this fotia from the gods. Now, if you'll excuse me, I have to meet a friend down on earth."

Prometheus tried to fly away, but I stopped him.

"Thief!" I cried.

Prometheus slapped me across the face. I punched him. Prometheus tried to grab free from my reach. It was useless. He stayed stuck in my grip.

"Tell me why you are afraid of me," I demanded.

Prometheus groaned. "Fine," he said. "I am the Titan of Frontida. So, therefore, I can see your mellontikos. All that I can see for you is that you will bring only pain to my oikogeneia. Our oikogeneia."

Now it was my turn to be puzzled. He referred to me as family.

"What do you mean, our family?"

The Titan only shrugged, and I loosened my grip.

"How?" I asked.

Prometheus did not answer.

"I must be going now. Antio sas! " he said.

The Titan ran away from me. I looked up. A new figure was approaching, only this time he was smaller, about my size. He had a

simple mustache and black jeans. He also wore a belt and a red vest. His hair was combed back, and lightning flickered out of his eyes. I was terrified.

"HAVE YOU SEEN A TITAN CALLED PROMETHEUS?" he bellowed.

This guy is loud.

"Uh—No?" I lied. *After all, what harm could this person do to me?*

The man grabbed my throat. His eyes turned a light blue. Then he started glowing. I'm surprised he didn't slice my head off on the spot.

"DON'T LIE TO ME, BOY! I SAW HIM COME DOWN HERE JUST A MINUTE AGO! WHERE IS HE??" he snapped.

"Why should I tell you?"

"BECAUSE I AM THE KING!"

"Of what land?" I asked.

The man growled.

"Who are you?" I asked.

"I AM ZEUS," he snapped, "KING OF THE GODS! YOU IRRITATE ME WITH YOUR IGNORANCE. I SHAN'T WASTE MY STRENGTH ON A PUNY CHILD LIKE YOU!"

Zeus stopped choking me and ran off after Prometheus.

Then, suddenly, I started falling again. The wind against my swollen foot hurt. I was in pain. I started to see land. I cheered. My foot hurt from the impact.

Slowly, I stood up. I seemed to be in a garden. There were four gardeners tending to the plants. I looked behind me. A man a little bigger then Prometheus was holding a massive shell. There were clouds in the shell. It was the sky. The man wore a black tank top, black jeans, and a black belt. (No, it wasn't a karate belt.) His shirt and pants had little doodles of planets, stars, and galaxies. His face had weird tattoos on it. Also, he had messed up short hair and was barefoot.

"Yo!" the man yelled. He smiled and looked at me.

Now, at this age, I was still fairly shy.

"Uh–hello??" I said.

"I'm Atlas! You can call me Mr. Awesome!" he yelled excitedly.

"You look like someone I met earlier this morning. He said his name was Prometheus," I recalled.

A look of worry spread across the Titan's face.

"Prometheus is my brother. Was he joggin' from a big dude?" Atlas asked.

"He said he had a friend to meet down on earth," I answered.

Atlas frowned.

"Who?" he asked.

"I don't know," I said. *Because I didn't*!

"What else did he say?" Atlas asked.

"Nothing," I lied.

"That meddler's gonna get himself into some serious trouble someday." Atlas stared at me for a long time.

I looked down.

"There's somethin you ain't telling me," Atlas frowned.

"He was running from someone named Zeus," I babbled.

"It's as I feared. He had a plan to do somethin' for a long time, and he wouldn't tell it to me. He betrayed the gods." Atlas frowned again.

I stared at the ground

"What's wrong?" Atlas asked.

"Nothing," I lied.

"I bet you're wonderin' why I'm holdin' the sky," Atlas said.

"Yep," I confessed.

"Well, here's your answer, kid. Long story," Atlas hissed.

I shook my head. *That was no answer! Anyway, I had to find my family. Atlas could help…right? I mean, he seemed to be a really nice guy.*

"Do you know anyone here who knows a lot?" I asked.

"In that garden, there's a tree. By the tree, there is a dragon named Ladon. He knows the answers to most stuff I ask him. He should be fine. " Atlas replied.

I walked into the garden. The gardeners scowled at me. I kept walking until I came to an grapefruit tree. A dragon was sitting by the tree, munching happily on a grapefruit. I was a bit scared at first, but the fact that the dragon wasn't trying to eat me made it so I wasn't scared anymore.

This is definitely Ladon, I thought.

He had thick, bushy hair and was really long. He was like a snake with legs. Smoke fluttered out of his nostrils.

"Can I help you?" Ladon asked.

"Yes. I'm Hephaestus. I was told you could help me."

"With what?"

"Piecing together my past."

"Ah, I see. Let me guess. You somehow lost all your memories except your name?"

How smart is this guy?

"Wow. You're prophetic," I exclaimed.

Ladon and I chatted for a bit, but neither of us knew how I lost my memories. After a long talk, we sat by a tree. Ladon slithered away from me for a bit.

"I need to check on Atlas," Ladon said.

Five minutes later, Ladon returned.

"Come on, kid. We're going on a trip." Ladon started walking.

"Why?" I asked.

"Because," Ladon turned around. "I think I know who your family is."

I grabbed some fruits and started walking.

"Wait for me!" Ladon said.

Ladon and I walked for a few days without rest. We finally stopped in a forest outside of a town Ladon called Olympia. We got there pretty late, so we rested for the night. When I woke up, I heard voices

"Who is he?"

"Is he one of us?"

"Get Mama!"

I opened my eyes. Four children were standing above me. They all looked about my age. Two boys and two girls. One boy was quite handsome. He had shiny, wavy hair. He was wearing a large trench coat. Quite fancy. One girl was blonde and had a dress with designs of flowers on it. She was quite beautiful. The other girl wore a battle helmet, armor, and boots. She held a sword and bow was on strapped onto her back. The second boy had long hair that stuck straight up. He had a blank red T-shirt and also wore jeans and shoes. He was hovering a couple inches above the ground. He also wore a cape.

I stood up. "Who are you?" I asked.

"We're the gods! Well, the young ones, anyway. She's Persephone, he's Hermes, that's Athena, and I'm Apollo. Who are you?"

"My name is Hephaestus."

"Hephaestus? That can't be your name. There's only one Hephaestus in this world, and he's dead," Apollo said.

I wasn't dead!

"You must have mistaken me for a different Hephaestus. I am most definitely alive," I reassured.

Ladon woke up just then.

"Hey guys! I assume you've met Hephaestus?" Ladon said.

"Yes, sir!" Apollo answered.

"Is this who you thought my family was? They don't look a lot like me," I said.

Ladon ignored me.

"Children, is Hecate here? We need to ask her something," Ladon said.

"Yes, she's here. I'll go get her," Persephone said. Persephone ran off.

Ladon turned back to me. "Hephaestus, we need Hecate to do a memory reveal. A memory reveal is when someone shows someone else's memories to you. The spell is not painful," Ladon said.

Persephone returned with a tall woman who had a feral cat with her. She wore a demonic crown, a cape with a collar, and dress that covered her feet. She also had an amulet with a symbol carved into it. The cat purred.

"Hello, Hephaestus. I am Hecate. How do you do?" Hecate greeted me.

"How do you know my name?" I asked.

"Hecate knows all. Are you ready for the operation?"

"Uhhh… sure?"

"Fantastic! Now I need you and Apollo to sit on the grass next to each other."

Apollo and I sat next to each other. Hecate started saying a bunch of words like connectius and memorius. Then a golden light tunnel appeared, connecting my head to Apollo's head. Suddenly, I started seeing visions of Apollo as a little boy, playing with his family. I saw another vision of Apollo playing with Persephone, Hermes, Athena, and… me!

After that the tunnel turned a dark red. I saw a vision of Apollo playing with me, but this time a man appeared and grabbed me. I looked closely at the man, but I couldn't tell who it was. Next the tunnel turned golden again, and I saw the events that occurred throughout the night. Deer and owls moved through the area. Then the tunnel disappeared, and Apollo got up.

"I… I… I'm your brother. That kid in those memories, that was me!" I exclaimed.

"I was trying to tell you that!"

"That man, in the vision, who was he?"

"That man, Hephaestus, was our father, Zeus. He didn't want me and you playing together because he was ashamed of you because of your foot. I couldn't heal it, so he threw you out the palace window. His intention was your death," Apollo lamented.

"Why?"

"He thought that you would never be worshiped by the townspeople because of your foot. So he threw you out."

"What do you mean, 'worship'?"

"Hephaestus, you're a god."

"What!?"

"Yep. We're gods. No joke. Hate to say it, but we gotta go home now. Mom wants us home for dinner," Apollo said gloomily.

"Why can't I come with you?"

"Uhh… you know what, you're family. I think it's time for you to come home."

I bade Hecate farewell and went with the other gods. We exited the forest and hiked up a very tall mountain to get back.

What a workout.

I finally saw a palace at the top of the mountain, and when we got there, we walked in.

"Home, sweet home," Apollo said happily.

A woman walked into the room and hugged Apollo. She wore a long green dress and had long blonde hair.

"Mom, this is Hephaestus. He's our brother," Apollo said excitedly.

The woman saw me. She put her hand over her mouth. She started to cry.. Then she came over and hugged me.

"Hephaestus…it's… it's you. You came home. Apollo, he's… he's been so sad since you were exiled. We all have. But now…you're home. Come! We must eat. Dinner's on the table!" she exclaimed.

We all sat down for dinner. I told them my story.

"Wow. That's… that's really sad. Zeus won't be home for a while, but when he does get home, we all need to have a further discussion on this matter." Hera finished eating her steak.

The rest of dinner was pretty quiet. After dinner, Zeus got home.

"Hello, Dad," I said.

"WHO ARE YOU?" he bellowed.

"I'm your son. I saw you a few weeks ago when you were chasing Prometheus."

"Oh, now I remember. GET OUT!"

"Dad, this is my home. I think I'll stay."

Zeus growled. Just then, Hera walked in.

"Hello, honey. I see you are chatting with our son," she said.

"WHY IS HE HERE! I THOUGHT THAT I GOT RID OF HIM! " Zeus said.

"Honey, he's family. Explain to him what you did."

"Ugh. FINE! Hephaestus, before I threw you out the window, I stole your memories and put them in a jar. It's in the kitchen cabinet," Zeus mumbled angrily

Hera walked over to the cabinets and looked around. When she turned around, she held a glowing jar.

"That's the one!" Zeus sighed, angrily.

Afterwords, I drank my memories, which retrieved them, then Zeus and I made amends. (He even stopped yelling so much!). He let me choose something to be the god of, and I chose the forge. So now I live on Olympus with my family. (Well, and my Uncle Hades dog, Cerbie.).

THE END

Finding Poetic Voice

Tasslyn Magnusson worked with Inés Garcia in revision to highlight Inés' own poetic voice in her poem, *I Am Just Some Latina*.

Dear Reader,

I'm going to tell you a secret. Poets often use a line from another poet or poem. Sometimes you see them as epigrams (italics at the beginning of a poem) and sometimes you'll see an endnote. This is a great poetic tool to use for inspiration or as writing prompts. And it's always important to acknowledge that other poet (see endnote). Sometimes, that original prompt is great, but you need to strike out on your own and find your voice. That is what Inés needed to do—follow the voice of her poem.

With *I Am Just Some Latina*, Inés needed to find the heart and soul of her poem and we started to do that by stripping away her prompts from a Jonathan Reed poem. And then I asked her to write whatever she felt like—flowing from her own heart. No self-censor! No editing! Just write and write. She had so many ideas when she discussed her poem with me and this was a topic so close to her heart, basically I told her just to let the poem flow out of her.

And while she was doing that, I wanted her to read some other poets and poems I picked out for her. Sometimes poets are chroniclers and sometimes poets are people who call us to action, to listen to the world. I had a feeling that Inés was the latter.

We read—and I asked Inés to study these poems: First, *Let America Be America Again,* by Langston Hughes and think about his refrain; I asked her to read, *homage to my hips,* by Lucille Clifton and think about joy; finally, I asked her to read several poems by Elizabeth Acevedo—an Afro-Latina poet and a national poetry slam champion. Acevedo writes about identity and connects the intimate with the political. Acevedo's, *hearing that joe arroyo song at the ibiza nightclub 2008,* is a model for line breaks and white space.

Finally, one of the exciting things about Inés poem—and the Jonathan Reed poem she was inspired by—is they are reversos. That means the poem can be read from top to bottom and bottom to top and have completely different meanings. We talked about reversos and mirror poems and ways to help the reader see what you are doing.

Inés—congratulations on doing the work to nurture your own unique and amazing poetic voice. I can't wait to see what else you will write! The world needs your voice.

Happy Writing!

Tasslyn Magnusson

Tasslyn Magnusson received her MFA in Creative Writing for Children and Young Adults at Hamline University in Saint Paul, MN. Her poems have been published or are forthcoming in *Broad River Review*, *Room Magazine*, *The Mom Egg Review*, *The Raw Art Review: A Journal of Storm and Urge*, and *Red Weather Online*. Her chapbook, *defining*, from dancing girl press was published in January 2019. She lives in Prescott, WI with her husband and two kids and two dogs.

Inés Garcia

Inés Garcia is a rising sophomore at Henry M. Gunn High School. From a young age, she has been an avid reader, her favorite poets being Pablo Neruda and Emily Dickinson. This year, she was published in Pandora's Box, her high school's literary magazine. Her poem, *I Am Just Some Latina* was inspired by her love for her Mexican heritage. In her free time, she enjoys running, snowboarding, listening to music, and walking her dog, Benito.

Tasslyn Magnusson: What changed and how much changed when you revised?

Inés Garcia: I worked a lot on structure. I decided to go with the reverso where the lines are the transitions themselves. The whole thing changed! I added in lines and took out old ones. That shifted the entire impact of the poem and created a more personal poem. I found my voice.

Q: Did you think you'd change stuff?

A: I knew there would be revision—but I hadn't seen the potential in my poem until we (my mentor and I) started talking. After that, I knew this poem could be more personal and powerful with some work.

Q: What advice to you have for Young Inklings who don't like revision?

A: Revision is hard but know that the end is always worth it. Sometimes you've got to sit down and read your poem or short story with fresh eyes and an open mind and be willing to completely change anything. Be willing to say, I really like this draft, but now that I look at this it could be greater.

Q: When did you start writing?

A: I started writing when I was in the 3rd grade. I had a teacher who had a daily writer's workshop—we'd write responses in our notebooks. She'd write back to me, in my notebook, telling me I had potential and such good vocabulary. She'd read out loud to us and then say, "You know who this author reminds me of—YOU!" I remember when she said my writing reminded me of Patricia Polacco—that made me feel special and seen and that I could be a writer.

Q: Why do you enjoy writing?

A: It's my favorite means of expressing myself. When I started writing for myself, I realized what kind of impact words could have. How I could describe feelings that I didn't think could exist. I could take my thoughts and express myself in ways I didn't know were possible.

Sometimes just putting the pencil to page I can start recognizing my feelings—oh, I'm feeling sad today. Writing down my emotions and finding ways to describe my feelings really helps.

Q: Where do you like to write?

A: At our kitchen table. We've had it since I've seven. Hardwood table. I'll sit on the bench and once I start writing I can't stop. The family is centered around that table. That's the table where I best express myself. Sometimes my best and hardest memories.

Q: How do you come up with ideas?

A: I'll get inspiration from the weirdest things. I'll read a poem and like somebody's ideas or a conversation about something in the news and I'll write it down. I'll ride my bike and I'll start elaborating and before you know it, I've created a poem.

Q: What are your favorite books to read?

A: I will read anything. But I love realistic fiction like *THE HATE U GIVE*. It's an important book and offered me a perspective of what I've had no idea about. I've never even thought about before. The books that open my mind and make me feel.

Q: Are you working on new poems?

A: Kind of. I always have an idea for a poem at the back of my mind. When I write it down, it's really rewarding. There's always a snippet of a line in my mind.

Q: Anything else you want to tell Young Inklings?

A: Know that you always have a story to tell. You always have a story and it may not be the story that everyone else is telling, but it's your story. There's a 100% guarantee that someone out there needs to hear it.

It might hard to write—I know you have a story to tell—and you should tell it.

I Am Just Some Latina

by

Inés Garcia

I am just some Latina

And I do not conclude that
I can follow my dreams into that beautiful blue *cielo*.
This may come as a shock, but
Society's stereotypes do not define you
Is a falsehood

I am bound for bitter-tasting realities; sugar skulls without sugar

I realize that now.
Following the status quo
Is more important than
Writing your own *destino*

Someone once told me
"You can do or be anything, and defy the cliché story that you were told to live"

Success is a *mamey* on the highest branch: tantalizing and unreachable.

I do not believe]
My dreams of giving my *café* colored brothers and sisters their own Renaissance will come true.

In the end,
We will be nothing but mere specks of dust, drifting in America's shining, blinding light.

Never again can it be said
We can rise up, and dazzle Them with our vivacious, colorful culture

It will be apparent that
We are forgotten, forbidden from sampling the sweet nectar that They call the American Dream

Only fools say
We have a chance of defying Them, and their sharpened words that pierce our skin like *lanzas*

***

This narrative will never change, **unless we reverse it.**